THE
MIDDLE
OF
NOWHERE

The Middle of Nowhere
© 2011 Stephen Brooke

ISBN 978-1-937745-00-4

Arachis Press is a small publisher dedicated to providing meaningful literature for all ages. Visit our site for more information and other books by Stephen Brooke.

4803 Peanut Road
Graceville, FL 32440
http://arachispress.com

THE MIDDLE OF NOWHERE

Stephen Brooke

Arachis Press 2015

stuck in the middle of nowhere

Chapter 1

"It's not much of a hill," I whispered to Dad.

Mr. Akin heard me. "That's about as big as they get around here," he said, "but it gives a great view of the river." Leave it to a real estate agent to turn the conversation into a sales pitch.

He pulled his car into the bumpy driveway and asked if we were ready for a look.

And that is how I ended up living in the middle of nowhere.

~

Yesterday, we'd been at home, back in Atlanta, on vacation. Dad taught high school, so he usually had free time in the summer. He liked to spend it fishing. I think he wanted to be a marine biologist at one time but ended up teaching general science and remedial math.

Mom had the title of vice-president at a local bank. That sounds important but, I guess, really isn't. She said the main difference between her and a teller was that she got to work longer hours.

Anyway, they were both borderline burn-outs. Mom didn't see much chance of advancement in her job and Dad knew he was stuck in a dead end. Not that he disliked teaching but he'd been trying to shove the same material into kids' heads for way too long. I can imagine how boring fraction review must get after ten or twelve years.

Then, one evening, as Dad was reading a fishing magazine, he leaned over to Mom and pointed at something in the back pages. She took a look and nodded.

"Let's check it out," she said.

I was curious, but didn't let on. I just kept watching TV like I'd noticed nothing. When Mom and Dad turned in, I opened the mag to see what had caught their eye. It took a while to find it but there, in the classified section, was a circled ad.

"For Sale: Hilltop Lodge," it went, "Motel, Restaurant and Marina on the banks of the beautiful Ruby River, just three miles from the Gulf of Mexico," and then continued with a price (which

I thought was way out of my folks' range) and the number of a real estate agent.

My dad was always planning fishing trips he wouldn't have the time or money to take, so I had no problem finding a Florida road map. Ruby was on the west coast, well north of the Tampa area. As far as I could tell, there wasn't much of anything there; it was a long way from any real city

My parents didn't waste any time. Next morning, Mom, who's the business-minded person in this family, called Mr. Akin, the real estate guy, got some info, talked with Dad, and called Akin back to set up an appointment for the following day. If I hadn't already clued myself in, I might have completely missed what was going on. That evening, Dad and I loaded up for an overnight trip to Florida.

Mom couldn't get away. Neither could my brother, Jeff, who had a summer job. It was going to be just Dad and I. Honestly, I wasn't crazy about this trip. I don't like to fish and I hate sudden changes of plan. Sitting at my computer sounded much better to me than sunburn, motion sickness, and all the other attractions of travel. But Dad was excited and I knew he wanted someone to go with him. I could put up with a day or two of father-son bonding.

We estimated a seven hour drive, down the Interstate and then over to the coast. I wouldn't even start to learn to drive for another year so it had to be Dad behind the wheel, all the way. He'd grabbed a short nap, earlier, and never pushed hard when he drove; plenty of rest stops with Dad. He could handle the drive without me to help him stay awake. After the first couple hours, it was all flat, uninteresting country and too dark to see much, anyway. I dozed off while we were still in Georgia.

It was just starting to get light when I awakened. We had pulled into a rest area somewhere. Dad was outside, leaning against a fender.

"Hey, I guess I woke you up."

I grunted in reply. I don't wake up easily.

Dad paid no attention. "I stopped here a couple hours back for some sleep. I was in cleaning up a bit and getting a snack." He held up some vending-machine junk food. "Want to use the facilities before we go?"

I slid out of the car and stood there, stiff and sleepy, on the pavement. Stretching, I asked Dad, "How far is it, now?"

"An hour away, maybe an hour and a half," he replied. "Depends on what the roads are like when we leave the Interstate."

"Okay, I'll be ready in a minute."

"No hurry, Martin. There's plenty of time. We're not expected until around ten."

Crossing the parking lot to the rest rooms, I could feel that things were different here. It was awfully warm for that early in the morning and the air carried a whole different bunch of smells than I was used to. Hey, Toto, we're not in Georgia anymore and I'm not sure why!

As soon as I finished inside and grabbed a soda from the cooler, we were on our way. It was only a few minutes to our exit. Soon, we were heading west, four lanes at first, then two. The traffic thinned quickly as we traveled on, the sunrise at our backs.

After a while, Dad spoke. "Look at the map, will you? There should be some little towns along this road."

I already had it open and folded back. I scanned the map for a moment. "There's one coming up in a mile or two," I replied. "A highway intersection, too."

"We cross a couple main roads, don't we?"

"Umm—" I looked again. "Yeah. There's another town after this one." We were just entering the outskirts of a little country town: a few houses, a convenience store. "Here comes the highway, now."

They even had a traffic light. Another minute and we were in open country again.

"After the next town," I continued, "We reach Nineteen. That's a four-laner." I paused before adding "It's the last highway before the coast."

Dad nodded. "We have to turn south, there."

I looked out the window. We were passing a patch of scrubby woodland. "This is an ugly kind of place."

"Yeah." He smiled. "It was prettier back along the Interstate. They don't have much in the way of soil, close to the coast."

"It looks like it's just white sand," I observed. "We aren't passing many farms, now."

"The main crop where we're headed is pine trees."

I knew that. I'd read up on the area.

"And," added Dad, with a grin, "fish."

He glanced over. "But I know you don't care much about that." Then he went all serious on me.

"Things may change a lot for all of us, you know. Pretty quickly, too."

"Are you really planning to buy a motel? I mean, can you afford it?" I asked. I had intended to play it cool but I couldn't hold my questions any longer.

"We can put a good bit down; your mother's good at saving money. One way or another, we should be able to make a deal. If," he continued, "the place is worth it."

"Why do you and Mom want to move way out in the 'boonies'? I thought you liked Atlanta." They were always saying what a great city it was.

I thought it was a good place to live, too. There's a lot going on in a big city and I was just getting old enough to check it out on my own.

Dad didn't say anything right away. After a while, he spoke.

"Nothing was happening for your mom and me back in Atlanta." Then he chuckled. "We were stuck in a rut on the road to nowhere!"

Dad can't help it. He's naturally goofy.

"Anyway," he continued, "we needed a change and the bigger the better."

We rode for a while without speaking, as I fiddled with the radio. One oldies and a couple country stations came in, none of them very clearly. It seemed like we were a long way from anything; like *we* were on the road to nowhere.

~

Eventually, we hit Highway Nineteen. There wasn't even a town at this intersection, just a convenience store. Dad stopped for gas and to make sure of his route. He also stocked up on Twinkies and coffee. I had another soda. That's about all my stomach will tolerate when I travel.

We would follow this highway for a while, until we could turn west again. Both sides of the road were planted, mile after mile, with pine trees. They weren't kidding about the main crop here. The county was even named Pinelands!

A weathered hand-painted sign (some local thought that he or she was an artist) read "Visit Beautiful Ruby, the Jewel of the Wild Coast. Turn Here." So we did and found ourselves on a meandering country road. At first, we passed through alternating patches of pines and swamp land. I found out later that the road ran more or less parallel to the Ruby River.

That gave way to low sand hills. I began to see some homes; there was a mix of trailers and old-fashioned, tin-roofed Southern houses.

Then, topping a hill, we saw the river, a bridge, a town. We had reached Ruby.

Chapter 2

To make a short story even shorter, we crossed the river (it was wide here, close to the Gulf), found Mr. Akin's office, and all got into his car to go see the property.

The Hilltop Lodge was up the river a mile and a bit, which put it toward the edge of town. Ruby was strung out along the south side of the water. Across the bridge, the way we had come in, was a smaller village named Akinville.

Mr. Akin explained that his family had been early settlers of the area and that there were Akins all over the place. He said we should just call him Wally to avoid confusion. Wally was a big, easy-going sort of guy, and very much a "good ol' boy."

I was not impressed by either the motel or the town and my expectations had been pretty low to begin with. Actually, I'd hoped that it might be some sort of tacky but picturesque resort. This could have been any boring little town.

The Lodge *was* on a hilltop of sorts. There were ten rooms and a small restaurant arranged along a curved drive. Across the road were some RV spaces and docks, on a short channel leading to the river. It was stretching it to call it a marina.

As we got out, I told Dad, "There isn't anyone staying here!"

He looked around and nodded. "It's past check-out time, I think," he answered in a low voice. "There may be some guests later." He didn't sound concerned; Dad was already in love with the place.

Mr. Akin—Wally—took us in to meet the owners. They were an older couple, planning to retire. I didn't catch their names but I looked at the legal papers, later, and saw that they were the Lesters.

Anyway, Mr. and Mrs. Lester, who originally came from the North, had run the motel for something like fifteen years. But the place had been around a lot longer than that; the sign out front said "since 1948." It looked old, too, and in need of repairs. Patching it up would keep us busy.

For that matter, it occurred to me that just the "day to day" of a motel might mean quite a bit of work. Not if the place was always as empty as this, though.

Dad never asked how much business the Hilltop Lodge did. He didn't have to; the Lesters had all the information ready for him. They were awfully eager to sell. I reckon they were simply tired of being tied down. Running a motel requires so much of your time. It turned out that they were usually filled up on weekends, at least at this time of the year. There would be rooms available tonight, if we wanted to stay, but tomorrow guests would start arriving for a long Fourth of July holiday.

Wally said this was probably their busiest time of the year but not necessarily the most profitable. "Parties of fishermen are where you make the money," he informed us. "Not families on vacation."

~

Dad decided we might as well spend the night and get to know the area. Neither of us felt like taking the long trip home without rest. After Akin returned us to his office, we got into our car and drove around. There was a nice restaurant, down near the mouth of the river; they only did breakfast at the Hilltop. I have to admit, it was scenic along the river, even if the town wasn't much.

Later, we checked into the Lodge. We sat on the dock and watched the gulls as the sun set. I'd brought some paper and I tried to sketch. I hope to be an artist, someday, but couldn't turn out anything worthwhile, *that* day.

One thing I can say about Ruby is that it's quiet, even on the main road. Nothing disturbed us all night.

The next morning we had breakfast there at the Hilltop, Dad scarfing down the grits and sausage gravy, me with some toast. Wally Akin came in and sat with us. There weren't any other customers in the restaurant.

He ordered a cup of coffee and, after some pleasantries, got down to business.

Dad did his best not to seem too interested. He said he'd think about it and discuss it with his wife and if they were interested they'd call and so on. I couldn't help smiling at that. Dad's just not very good at hiding his feelings. Wally caught my expression and gave a little smile of his own. There was a definite twinkle in his eye, as the cliché goes. We both knew Dad was hooked. But I wasn't.

~

All the way home, I thought about what this would do to my life. There would be changes, I knew, and lots of them, but I was pretty hazy on the details. Dad was feeling good and I didn't want to bring him down with my concerns. I wasn't sure I could put them into words, anyway. First, I needed to work some of this out by myself. I'd chew on it a while to see what flavor it was.

The month that followed brought change after change. Did I mention that I don't like changes? Mom and Dad had driven down to Ruby the very next weekend and signed a contract. I think Mom liked it even better than Dad. Maybe it was the idea of running her own business. There was an entrepreneur inside Mom, just waiting to get out.

The deal was worked out and finalized, finances and all, in practically no time. We planned to move down in mid-August. Jeff could help a lot before he entered college in Athens. I wished he'd switched to a school closer to our new home.

We were all winding things up in Atlanta. Mom gave notice at the bank and Dad didn't renew his contract. I had to say goodbye to a few friends from school, but there weren't that many people I'd miss.

Rita was one I really would miss. She was my guitar teacher. Two afternoons a week, I'd go to her little studio in the back of a music store and take classical guitar lessons. There wasn't likely to be a classical instructor near Ruby and certainly not one that could replace Rita; she was in her twenties and had long black hair. When we said goodbye, she told me I could e-mail her if I ever needed help with my music studies.

Before I knew it, we were packing things up and had a "for sale" sign in the yard. A Realtor began parading clients through our half-empty house. It sold soon after we moved out.

Chapter 3

August is a busy month for Ruby. That's scallop season in Florida and hordes of visitors come to the coast to search for the shellfish. Dad had already been spending some of his time in Ruby, to get the hang of running the Lodge, while the rest of us prepared for our move. With the crowds of scallopers in town, we all had to jump right into it.

Five o'clock, the first morning, Dad wakened us. There were living quarters above the restaurant; Jeff and I shared a room.

"We open for breakfast at five-thirty," he said. "You guys can help."

Jeff jumped out of bed, all ready to go. I hate my brother, sometimes. "Is Mom up?" he asked.

"She's already prepping, downstairs."

The bathroom was claimed by Jeff, as usual, but I didn't care. I don't need a long time to get going in the morning, once I'm out of bed. I'm pretty good at working out an efficient routine and can get things done quickly.

"Always give a hard job to a lazy man," my dad likes to say. "He'll find the easiest way to do it."

I take that as a compliment. I suspect that this country was made great by lazy people who figured out the best way to get things accomplished, not by hard work like I hear all the time!

That was a week day, so breakfast wasn't much trouble. Even on busy mornings, it didn't really seem hard, once we got a routine going. It was a pretty small place; with Jeff and I assisting, Mom could handle it but she said she might have to hire someone after school started.

I'm sort of a neat-freak and everyone knows it, so the job of cleaning motel rooms naturally fell to me. There are a lot of chores that need attending in a place like the Hilltop Lodge, especially on busy weekends. Someone has to manage the "marina." That means selling bait, fishing licenses, sodas, and so on from the little shop by the docks. It also means keeping an eye on our launching ramp and charging a couple bucks for every boat that goes in. On a big Saturday, that can add up to a good bit of money. It can be quite a bit of work, too. Dad took charge of that operation.

~

Down by the dock stood a little open shed. "What's that for?" I wondered, the first time I saw it. When I walked over, though, the odor clued me to its purpose. It was a fish cleaning station.

I could have made some major money cleaning the catch but it's really nasty work. Also, you end up doing it in the evening, usually, and sometimes well into the night, when the air is full of carnivorous insects. Not to mention the possibilities of dismemberment that go with wielding a sharp knife! I was willing to leave it to a pro.

Our first afternoon, Wally Akin came by. He was accompanied by a plump, middle-aged woman and a girl.

"This is Betty Akin," he said. "Another one of us."

"Pleased to meet you," said Betty, shaking my parents' hands. "I've been handling the fish cleaning for the Lodge. I'd be glad to keep on, if you want."

"Oh, yes," Mom replied. "The Lesters gave us your number. We can just call when we need you?"

"That's right, ma'am. You can almost always reach me in the afternoon." She turned to the blonde girl beside her. "This is my daughter, Amy. Your boy will likely be going to school with her."

"Hi," said Amy. She was kind of cute, though a tad chunky, and seemed shy. Little did I know! It turned out she was just being polite around the adults.

"Hello, Amy. Why don't you and Martin get acquainted?" Mom turned to Betty and Wally. "Won't you come in?"

The adults trooped into the restaurant, which doubled as the office, leaving Amy and me outside.

I hate it when they do that. I mean, stick you with someone you don't know. I had no idea what to talk about but Amy talked enough for both of us. Even if I'd wanted to, I couldn't have said much.

THE MIDDLE OF NOWHERE

Amy told me about the school situation here. She was just entering the ninth grade and was all excited about going to high school. Gee, we tenth graders are already jaded, I guess. Anyway, we'd assumed I'd attend school in Nelson, because Ruby is in the same county.

The Ruby River is the dividing line between two counties, Hancock to the south and Pinelands to the north. Kids in Hancock go to school in Nelson, which is almost forty miles from Ruby. The high school at Blessed is only half the distance. So, students from Ruby are allowed to attend school in Pinelands, the same as their friends across the river in Akinville. Most of *them* had crossed the county line to attend elementary and middle school in Ruby.

I decided right then that I was going to attend school in Blessed. It would mean a much shorter bus ride. When Dad heard the reason for my choice, he said, "Good, that'll give you more time to work." Very funny, Dad. But Mom and Dad did okay the switch.

I think Amy liked me, if only because I was someone new and older than her and didn't interrupt much. She was glad I decided to go to the same school, also. Amy was nice enough and nice looking, too, but not the type I usually hang with. I hope I don't sound like some sort of snob. I try not to.

It's just not in my nature to be outgoing and everyone's buddy. I have to watch my mouth sometimes, too. Like the line goes, if you can't say something nice, don't say anything at all, so I don't talk that much.

~

School starts early around here. I had a little more than a week of summer vacation left.

Chapter 4

Dad already owned a little aluminum boat but the deal for the Hilltop had included Mr. Lester's twenty-three footer. The old man had been a fishing guide, on the side. There were other guides who operated out of our marina and they charged plenty. Plus, they got to be called "Captain" and it's just plain a cool way to make a living. Dad immediately signed up for the Coast Guard course so he could be a captain, too.

This was a slow Tuesday morning and, leaving Mom in charge (as if she isn't *always* in charge), Dad and Jeff and I got into the skiff to go try our luck at scalloping. Since scallops live out in the Gulf, we first had to negotiate three miles of river. That takes a while in a small boat with a low-powered motor but it let Jeff and me get our first good look at Ruby's waterfront.

Dad had already been on the river, so he assumed the role of guide. A few really big houses were located on the upper river; a handful of well-to-do folks had "discovered" Ruby. Mostly, though, it was small homes, many used only on weekends, and water-related businesses. We certainly weren't the only marina or motel in town. There were also a couple of small seafood packers. They did mostly scallops and crabs, since Florida had banned most fish netting a while back.

Just a little below our own channel was a new resort development named 'The Mooring,' with pseudo-Cracker cottages. Much of the river bank, though, was still in its original state, woods or marsh. The marsh grass areas are supposed to be important to the environment and they keep the river looking wild and natural. They also provide a breeding place for the local variety of "no-see-um," the sand gnat. No-see-ums on steroids, I'd call 'em.

"What's that sound?" asked Jeff. "It sounds like a herd of donkeys!"

We were rounding a big bend in the stream, with wild growth on either side. It felt like we could have been a hundred miles from civilization. What Jeff had heard were cormorants, calling from their perches above the water. I swear, they bray like donkeys.

"Here comes the bridge," called Dad, from his seat in the stern. "It runs straight from here."

Now, the Ruby River widened and grew busier. It was halfway to being a bay here and there was a lot of salt in the water. Back at the Hilltop, the water was only slightly brackish, though it rose and fell with the tides.

The waterfront grew more crowded. "There's the Sea Breeze Marina." Dad pointed. "And the Best Bet." We slid under the bridge. It was recently erected, and high, replacing an older wooden structure. Part of that old bridge remained, standing along side like a pier. Naturally, there were folks fishing from it. Only a really tall vessel wouldn't be able to pass under the new span. A ship that size would find the river too shallow, anyway.

Over to our left, stood Parker's Restaurant, the best sea food place in town. Beyond it, river turned to Gulf. That doesn't mean we suddenly reached deep water and waves (yes, I was disappointed). Along this coast, the bottom drops off very gradually, with miles of shallow grass flats and sand bars extending into the Gulf. That's one reason the fishing is good here.

Those flats are the place to hunt scallops. You have to get out and wade around to find them nestled in the sand. Some people use rakes but that tears things up so it's a bad idea, ecologically speaking.

We were novices, but we eventually managed to fill a pail. It was well past noon when Dad looked at the horizon and said, "We'd better head in."

It rains on August afternoons. Not always, but pretty often. Summer storms, in and of themselves, aren't a big deal. Still, you don't want to be out on the Gulf during one; not in a small boat.

We were chugging toward the river as a wall of dark clouds came up rapidly behind us. Lightning would flash deep within it.

That's the biggest danger. There's no shelter from lightning strikes on open water.

~

I wondered, not for the first time and certainly not for the last, what I was doing in this place, as the first chilling wave of rain passed over us. None of us said much, except Dad mumbling a few unprintable words under his breath. What could we say?

It grew extremely dark for a while. We felt like the rain was blowing right through us. Our little, flat-bottomed boat bounced across the choppy seas, Dad trying to keep it headed in the right direction.

We were all scared; don't doubt it for a second. Yet, aside from the possibility of lightning, there really wasn't much danger. The shallow water prevents the development of waves. Even if our motor had conked out, the afternoon winds are generally onshore and wouldn't blow us out to sea. But we were new to this sort of thing.

Poor Martin! Only fifteen and doomed to a watery grave. Thoughts like that nibbled on the edge of my mind as I bailed rainwater with a paper cup. At the same time, it was, admittedly, rather exciting while it lasted.

For summer storms can go as quickly as they come. Soon, we were passing through nothing worse than the occasional light shower. We headed up river, wet, miserable, and more knowledgeable. By the time we got home, we were in a pretty good mood and could laugh about our misadventure. Maybe, I was even a little proud of myself and my family for getting through it.

"I'm glad I didn't have to bother the Coast Guard," joked Mom, but we could tell that she had been worried.

As we sat, prying scallops from their shells, I had some time to think. Next week I'd be taking another trip, onto uncharted waters. School started on Monday.

Chapter 5

One is faced with choices when stepping onto a bus. Where do you sit? With whom do you sit? Do you go all the way to the back, where the trouble makers usually hang out? Or stay up front, near the driver? It's good to have friends at both ends of a bus.

There would already be cliques. Most of these kids had been around each other for years. How would I know who was who and what was what? The only people I had met were Amy and some of her girlfriends and I wasn't going to sit down with them. Near them, maybe, so I'd seem friendly without being pushy.

My stop was near the beginning of the bus route. That meant a longer ride in the morning, though a shorter one after school. More importantly, I could have my pick of seats. I chose one toward the middle and waited.

As others got on, we eyed each other but didn't interact. Pretty soon, there were small clumps of friends sitting together. The bus was about half full when it picked up Amy and her friend, Tiffany; names like Tiffany and Courtney were as popular here as elsewhere, though no one had used them when my mom was a girl.

Amy walked back, plopped right down beside me and started chattering. Tiffany slid into the seat in front of us without saying a word. She was as quiet as Amy was talkative and they had been best friends since preschool.

Call me shallow, call me selfish: I was uncomfortable. Everyone on that bus was going to think of me as Amy's friend, maybe even her boyfriend. Once people have you pegged, it's hard to change your status.

I was a bit embarrassed by Amy's attention, anyway. How did *she* think of me?

We crossed the bridge to Akinville and picked up a handful there. A few more would get in along the road into Blessed. They looked like a fairly normal group, except for one thing.

Turning to Amy, I asked, "Aren't there any black kids?"

"Not in Ruby," she replied. "I guess there are lots in Blessed."

Tiffany looked like she wanted to say something but didn't want to break in. She was seriously shy. I know because I have that problem myself, some. I tried to give her an encouraging look, like I expected her to speak. You know, raised eyebrows and all of that.

"Too many red-necks. In Ruby, I mean," she said. "I think they make blacks feel uncomfortable—unwelcome."

I suddenly realized that these girls might never have gone to school with blacks before nor even had a black friend. Ruby really was the middle of nowhere.

~

"How did you get into this class?"

"Brains," I answered. I couldn't resist.

I was sitting in my second period class, Algebra II, and I was the only sophomore there. I'm *not* a math whiz even if the nickname 'Smarty Marty' did get attached to me back home. Or what used to be home. Anyway, it takes a lot of hard work for me to keep up.

The guy who'd asked looked like he couldn't decide whether or not that was funny.

"Not really," I continued. "We could take Algebra I in eighth grade where I used to go school. I got a head start."

Then class began and we didn't talk more. It did feel odd being the youngest one there. I hoped no one expected me to be some kind of genius. They'd be disappointed.

And, with any luck, that nickname wouldn't follow me here.

~

The first day of school went by without problems; a lot better than expected, I'll admit. As a tenth grader, I was still fairly limited in my choice of classes: one each of English, math, PE, social studies, and a couple of electives.

More variety is permitted for juniors and seniors but it didn't look like much was available. Pinelands High was a small school.

They didn't even offer art. The former art classroom had been converted to a computer lab years ago.

There *were* plenty of blacks at Pinelands, just as many as back in Atlanta. More Hispanics here, though, a lot of them from Mexican families. I didn't notice any particular racial thing going on but at lunch many of the black kids did tend to group together.

So did the "red-necks." That's a word I won't use again. It's really derogatory. I know these guys use it themselves but then blacks sometimes use the "N-word."

Anyway, they formed a definite subculture. Some of the kids called them "cowboys" because they liked to wear western style clothes. You know, cowboy boots, those gaudy rodeo shirts. That kind of thing. But most students at Pinelands looked like teenagers anywhere. Cable TV reaches even to Ruby.

~

"Good afternoon, Mrs. Cannon." It wouldn't hurt to be nice to the bus driver. Some kids act like they don't even see the driver when they board a bus.

She looked up and gave me a nod. "'Afternoon."

I took a seat in the second row, right side, since I'd be getting off early. That would make it easier to exit a crowded bus. A sandy-haired boy took the front seat, right ahead of me. He'd already been on the bus when I'd boarded in the morning.

He turned around to look at me. "Hi," he said. "You from the new family at the Hilltop?"

"Yeah," I answered, "I'm Martin."

"Robby." He held out his hand. Not many guys my age offer to shake.

Amy was getting on. I gave her the wave. She said "Hi," and went to sit further back with Tiffany and her other friends, but not without giving Robby a look. It seemed that my new acquaintance was some sort of Amy repellent.

In a subdued way, he was a "cowboy." In his case, I think it was simply what he was accustomed to wearing, not any sort of statement.

"I live up the river from you. Up close to the highway."

He meant Highway Nineteen, which ran through Blessed. Roads ran along both sides of the river, turning off Nineteen and connecting at the bridge in Ruby. The school bus started its route along the south road and then looped back around on the north side, the way Dad and I had first come. After it got back to Nineteen, the bus turned north and continued to Blessed, passing that little store where we had stopped for gas.

"Back one of those dirt roads?"

"Uh-huh. We've got five acres, right on the river."

"On the river? Can you get a boat to it?" I asked.

"Naw. We're above the Falls."

The "Falls" were really nothing but some rather unexciting rapids. But the river got too shallow there to allow anything to pass, except maybe a canoe, and then only in the rainy season.

Robby lived there with his extended family, all of them true Florida "crackers." His father drove a log truck, which is considered a prestigious job, at least in terms of pay. He'd been here all his life and knew everyone on the bus, including, of course, Amy.

"We've been in the same class ever since I was held back in third grade."

So Robby was my age. About the same height, too, but stockier. Most guys are; I'm wiry according to my mom. To be honest, I'd need more muscle to qualify as wiry.

~

"Here's my stop," said Robby. "I hope my mom's waiting. It's a good mile back to our house.

"Hey, see you tomorrow," he said and stepped off the bus. A pickup truck was parked by the road.

A few minutes later, I was home, too. I was already calling the Lodge "home," but I didn't know if it really was.

Chapter 6

Over the next two weeks, I became friendly with Robby and his best buddy, Frank Hanley. Frank immediately latched onto me because he was desperate to learn guitar. He wanted to be a rock star or something.

I showed him some chords and stuff he could practice. He'd ride over on his bike, clutching a cheap-o electric, and want to "jam." In fact, he spent a lot of after-school time at the Hilltop.

An e-mail to Rita brought some help. I mean, I didn't know beans about playing rock. She sent me back, of all things, surf music. Before long, Frank and I were both able to work our way through "Walk, Don't Run" on our respective instruments. The piece was surprisingly similar to some of the classical stuff I had studied.

It got me back into regular practice habits, too. With the motel and school work, I didn't have much extra time. I also had decided to take band and was learning a new instrument, the flute. Flute because that was what Jeff had played and we had one lying around the place.

"Frank needs a place to hang out, you know," Robby told me. I didn't know but I was sure Rob would fill me in. People always do when they say something like that. "He doesn't like being at home right now. Doesn't get along with his mom's latest boyfriend. Or with his mom, a lot of the time."

Just when you think you've got reasons to feel sorry for yourself, someone with real problems comes along and spoils it all.

~

I was getting into the flow of things—we all were—when Labor Day arrived. Along with July Fourth, Labor Day weekend brings the largest crowds to Ruby. There was even a festival to help attract the tourists. After this holiday, most visitors would be fishermen. They weren't interested in the town, just in the water.

On the last couple of days before the Labor Day break, Amy

had been telling everyone to come see her at the festival. I had to ask Robby what that was about.

"She'll be in the show. Amy thinks she's a country singer." He added, with a laugh, "But she can't carry a tune in a bucket." I thought that was a little meaner than necessary. Rob is somewhat scornful of Amy and her friends. Although he wouldn't use the word, he thinks they're pretentious.

"How's she get in, if she's so bad?" I wondered.

"Her uncle, Fred Akin, is the organizer and MC. He always lets her sing. But then," he admitted, "he'll let just about anyone perform that asks."

One good thing about these big holidays is that the motel guests generally book for the entire weekend. That meant I didn't have any major cleaning to do, just a quick freshening of the rooms and I'd be free. Jeff was around, too, so he could help.

Before eleven on Saturday morning, the day of the festival, I had finished my work and the restaurant was cleaned up. My folks had agreed that I could go check things out; I especially wanted to see the outdoor art show.

Frank had come by on his bike and was waiting for me. We pedaled off together toward the park. It was near the bridge, about a mile away.

That's a mile by bike, taking all the shortcuts. It would be a bit further if one stuck to the main road and further yet by boat. The river winds a good bit.

We heard music as we approached. A pretty decent country band had been hired for the festival; the amateurs would do their thing between sets.

This was actually my first time at the park; I'd only ridden by, before. Not that much went on there. The building, the "community center," got some use in the evenings: aerobics class, square dancers, that kind of thing. A long porch along one side served as an outdoor stage.

~

"That's Tiffany's mother," said Frank, pointing to a small, brightly-dressed woman carrying a clip board. She stopped to talk with each of the arts and crafts exhibitors.

"I take it she's one of the event organizers."

"Yeah," Frank replied, "she's, like, into all this community stuff."

We had dismounted (no riding inside the park) and were wheeling our bikes between the rows of displays. A lot of it was pretty cheesy: glue-together crafts, method painters, tee-shirt vendors. Here and there, some quality exhibits appeared. There were a couple of good jewelry makers, a potter, several wood-workers. Mostly, they used red cedar, which grows like a weed in this area.

"Hello, Frank." We had come even with Tiff's mother.

"Hi, Mrs. Theo." The name was actually Theophilopolous but everyone said "Theo," so I will, too.

She looked at Frank, expecting him to introduce me. He was oblivious. Social graces were not Frank's forte.

The easiest thing to do in these situations is to fall into polite patterns, however phony they may feel. "How do you do?" I said. "I'm Martin Groves." I even held out my hand.

She shook it and said, "So you're Martin. Tiffany has been telling me all about you."

Which left me a bit tongue-tied. I didn't know I'd made much of an impression on Tiffany. Really, I couldn't imagine her gushing about *anyone*. She seemed so self-contained.

"Oh, uh, tell her I said 'hello.'"

"She's around here somewhere, with Marlon. Why don't you boys go find them?" She turned back to her business with the vendors.

Marlon was Tiffany's older brother. We had a couple of classes together, algebra and band, although he was a junior. Marlon was bright, outgoing, active in school affairs and, perhaps, too self-consciously "intellectual." Having met his mom, I could see where he got it.

I had always hung with guys like Marlon in the past. Now, I wasn't sure that was where I belonged. He and his friends were pretty much like those I had known back in Atlanta but coming in new like this gave me a fresh look at things.

~

Tiffany sat by herself at a picnic table in front of the stage. I wasn't surprised that Marlon had ditched her. Older brothers do that.

"Hey," I greeted her, "anyone else around?"

She gestured toward the stage. Amy was part of a crowd milling around up there. The worried looking ones were probably the band, keeping an eye on their equipment.

"Oh," I said. "Is she on soon?" I sat down across the table from her.

"I guess." She looked like she wasn't going to say anything more, then changed her mind. "The band just finished playing."

"Yeah." I'd heard them but hadn't thought about it.

Frank was perched on the end of the table. "Check out the guitar. Epiphone Sheraton." Frank's favorite reading material was music catalogs.

"Uh-huh," I said. "Pretty." I smiled at Tiffany. She almost smiled back.

"That guy in 'Oasis' played one. Except his had an English flag painted on it."

"British," said Tiffany.

"Huh?" said Frank.

"It's a British flag, not English," she repeated. "It's for the whole United Kingdom."

"Whatever," agreed Frank.

I wanted to laugh but wasn't sure whether one or both might take offense.

Someone was at the mike. I turned around to watch, back against the table.

Frank slid down onto the seat beside me. "That's Pastor Fred," he told me. "Amy's uncle."

Pastor? I knew there were a half-dozen churches in town but we kept too busy on Sundays to attend one. Most of them struck me as a little too conservative for my parents, anyway.

Fred Akin was making some announcements: "Such-and-such car is blocking an entrance and so-and-so car had its lights left on and there are still plenty of raffle tickets and the fish fry will start in half an hour and we have a bunch of talented people who are going to perform for you and wasn't the band great? Let's give them another round of applause! And here's Grampa Somebody-another who's going to play his fiddle."

Then some old local sawed his way through a couple of traditional tunes. There was polite applause and the pastor returned to the microphone.

"Thank you, Grampa, that was wonderful and let's hear it for him, folks! And I want to thank you all for coming out today and isn't it a beautiful day? I hope it doesn't rain! And, by the way, you're all invited to our Methodist church tomorrow, services at ten and this next girl is a great little singer and only fourteen and let's give a big welcome to Amy Akin!"

He popped an accompaniment tape into a cassette deck and Amy stepped up to the mike. I can't say Amy was really good but she managed to stay on tune most of the time. Maybe she'd improved since Robby last heard her.

What she *did* do was over-sing something awful. Amy had a nice enough voice but seemed to think she needed more. She started adding all those tricks and embellishments that you hear too much of from girl singers.

I turned around and observed, "She, uh, kind of overdoes it, doesn't she?"

Tiffany gave a look like she didn't quite approve of me criticizing her friend. Then she laughed. "She thinks she's Reba McIntire."

I was beginning to like Tiffany.

~

More announcements and more wannabes followed. Amy came and joined us at the table, along with a couple of her girl friends. Everyone complimented her performance. After all, it takes nerve just to go on stage.

The band started up again. Frank wanted to get closer to the stage and the girls decided to find something to eat. I chose to take a more thorough look at the exhibits, so we went our different ways.

Chapter 7

"Impressionism," stated Marlon Theo.

Marlon wasn't really into art, though he thought he should be. He was trying to impress Melissa Parker (yes, of the restaurant Parkers) with his taste and knowledge.

Normally, I wouldn't butt in on a guy under those circumstances but Melissa—Missy to her parents, Messy to her friends—was his cousin, so it didn't matter. The girl knew he was full of himself, anyway.

She was a senior and worked evenings at the restaurant, saving her money for college. Now that I'd seen them both, I realized that Messy looked a lot like her aunt, Mrs. Theo. Tiffany and Marlon must take after their father.

Giving myself an authoritative air, I looked the pictures over and said, with mock solemnity, "*Expressionism.*"

Melissa caught on right away and fell into the spirit of it. "Ah, yes, but note the Fauvist use of color."

"And the subtle Cubist influences," I continued.

Marlon looked disgusted. He turned to the artist, sitting nearby; judging by his smile, he'd been listening.

"What do you call it, Mr. Edwards?"

"Sorry, Marlon, but I don't like the Impressionism tag. There haven't been any real Impressionists since the Nineteenth Century. Things move on, you know."

Apparently, this guy knew Messy and Marlon. I found out later that he supplemented his earnings as an artist by doing the substitute teacher bit. His wife taught, too, full time, at the elementary school here in Ruby. All the local kids had passed through her class. His hand-lettered sign read "Pat Edwards, Acrylic Paintings," and he was obviously the best artist at the show.

Mr. Edwards rose from his lawn chair. He was a short, muscly guy. I would have pegged him as an athlete, not an artist.

"The Impressionists were painting the world around them. It might have been their impression of the world but they were still after, um, a form of reality. My pictures are about my—" He searched for a word. "*Emotional* response to the world. In that sense, they're Expressionism. But," he added with a smile, "the result looks about the same."

"Martin's an artist," said Messy, gesturing toward me. I'd never told her that but things get around in a small town. Especially when you say them to Amy Akin.

"That right?" He seemed thoroughly unimpressed, while I was thoroughly embarrassed. Maybe he sensed it and that was why he was so nonchalant. Didn't want to put me on the spot.

"Yeah," I admitted. I didn't intend to volunteer more than that.

"Come by my studio, sometime, if you'd like. They," he nodded toward my companions, "can show you where." The artist turned to pick up a business card. "This has the address."

"Thanks." I pocketed the card. "Are you selling much?"

He chuckled. "No. Don't expect to, either, but I figure I should support the local show. It lets people know I'm around, if nothing else."

"My mom says that crafts are what sell," observed Marlon.

"Sure. Folks don't come to a show like this looking for fine art. But someone may pick up a card and think about it for a while and then drop by the studio. Or," he finished with a wry expression, "they may not."

"Okay, good luck, Mr. Edwards. See you around," said Marlon.

"And say 'hi' to Mrs. Edwards," added Melissa.

"'Bye, kids," replied the artist, settling back into his chair.

The three of us walked on a ways.

Messy spoke. "Mr. Edwards is really a nice guy."

"But a lousy teacher," retorted Marlon.

"Yes," she agreed. "He hates to discipline anyone."

"There's Frank," I said, waving to him. "I'd better go." I hadn't meant to intrude on them and thought I should use this excuse to get away.

"That kid is trouble," Marlon bluntly stated. "Why do you hang around with him?"

"He sort of attached himself to me. Hey, I get along with him all right. And," I added, "he's Robby's friend."

"Robby Dell? He's okay, for a red-neck (Marlon used the R-word, not me), but don't bring Frank if you come by my house. I don't like him around Tiffany."

"Don't be so negative, Marlon." Messy sounded exasperated; she'd had experience dealing with her cousin. "Tiff's got plenty of good sense. More than you!"

I said goodbye and left them then. It looked like they were still arguing as they walked off.

~

"Wanta get something to eat?" I asked Frank. "I'm paying."

"That's okay, I'm not very hungry."

"Hey, my dad handed me a twenty before we left. We might as well use it." I started toward one of the concession tents. Frank hesitated and then followed me. Of course, he hadn't brought much money.

That was why Dad had slipped me the twenty in the first place. We both knew Frank was usually short on cash. In two weeks, we'd practically adopted the kid.

We loaded up on disgustingly greasy food, washing it down with sodas. The band was playing a mix of country and Fifties rock while we ate.

"See what the bass player is doing?" asked Frank, as they chugged through "Kansas City." "That's called a 'walking bass.'" I knew that but I just nodded. "I never saw a chick play bass before. It's kinda cool, huh?"

"She's too old for you, man," I kidded. The bassist was a middle-aged woman, tall and thin. Attractive, too, in her hippie-musician way.

I swear, Frank actually blushed. With his complexion, it

showed and then some. "Aah," he said, "I didn't mean—oh, shut up."

"Okay, sorry." I smiled but I didn't tease him again.

A moment later, he blurted out, "Say, why don't you get a bass? We could do, like, a band thing."

That took me by surprise. "I already have two instruments to practice."

"Yeah, but a bass is just like a guitar, except bigger. You even play it with your fingers, same as your classical." Frank was serious about this. I wondered how long he'd been thinking along these lines.

The idea had, in fact, a certain appeal. "Let me give it some thought," I said. "A bass is pretty expensive, isn't it?"

"I'll show you some catalogs when we get home." *He* was calling the Lodge home, now, though he probably wasn't thinking about what he said. "'Course, you'll need an amp, too."

~

I was tired and sun burnt. I'd promised to be home early and it was threatening to rain, anyway. Labor Day probably isn't the ideal date to hold an outdoor show; an afternoon shower is practically guaranteed. Amy was going to do a couple or three more numbers so I decided to wait for that, then go as soon as she finished.

I kept an eye open for Robby but he'd been a no-show, so far. He hadn't been sure when, or if, he could get a ride into town.

A crowd of kids had gathered at the picnic tables. There were members of a square-dance club that had been whirling around below the stage. They still wore their nifty red-and-white checked costumes. People I knew from school were there, including several that lived in Blessed. There were younger brothers and sisters and grade school boys who wanted to hang with the older crowd. Some, I didn't know at all; they were the kids who went to school in Nelson. Amy and a bunch of her friends were huddled together.

33

About that time, Robby came ambling over from the road, where someone had let him out. The park was located beside the main road, on a piece of low land that ran down to the river. Some said it was *too* low and, one of these days, a hurricane would send water running through the community center. Rob greeted some of his friends and then came to sit by Frank and me. Amy had gone back up on stage.

Did you ever get that weird feeling like you're not really there? It's as if you've floated off and are watching everything from a distance. That's the way I was starting to feel. I was just beat, I guess, and had eaten too much of the wrong food.

Amy's voice was coming from the stage like a far-off radio. I found myself wondering why I was sitting there with Frank and Robby. Did I even like these guys? What was I doing here, anyway? I was sure I had something important to do but I couldn't remember what it was.

Then I went off and found a trash can and lost my lunch and things cleared up. I had an horrendous headache, though, and it got even worse pedaling home. Mom gave me some Ibuprofen and I went straight to bed.

~

Frank came by later, my folks told me, after I was asleep. He and Robby had seen me puke my guts and he was concerned. I had told them I was going home and I'd be okay and that Frank should stay. After all, Robby had just got there.

He rode over again, the next morning.

"Man, you really spewed," he told me. "It was totally disgusting."

I sort of grunted. I still wasn't feeling that great.

"Are you mad at me? Like, for not riding home with you or something?" He was genuinely worried about it. In a way, it was kind of pathetic but I was touched.

"Oh, no, no," I assured him. "I'm just cranky, sometimes, and I still have a headache." My headaches often lasted two or three days. Once in a while, they got bad enough to make me nauseous and, perhaps, to up-chuck. But there was no need to tell Frank that I was Mr. Migraine.

"Say, did you bring those catalogs?" I asked. "We can look at them after I finish the rooms—but you've got to help."

Chapter 8

I was an idiot, of course. Looking back, you see that kind of thing. Amy had been nice to me, the new kid, and I had hesitated. Not that I ever did anything remotely offensive, but my response *had* been pretty cool. Hey, I told you I have trouble being outgoing.

Now, she kind of ignored me; she was finding plenty of new friends at a new school. We still said "hi," and all that. I think she appreciated me coming to see her sing, too. She even joked about my response to her performance—she didn't know her voice was bad enough to make people puke.

Although I'm not sure, I suspect that line originated with Tiffany. Tiff appreciates sarcasm. She thinks of things like that but won't say them, except maybe to Amy or her brother. Usually, she just writes it down, which is smart. People who let their quips fly without thinking, like yours truly has once or twice, often end up in deep, uh, water.

But Amy was a sweet kid. Even those who thought she talked too much about nothing liked the girl. Even Robby. The only problem that existed between those two was Robby's lack of tact. He could be unnecessarily blunt.

Amy had probably given me a head start on trying to get along here. You know, people would see me and think "Oh, that's Amy's friend" instead of "Who's that geek?" But I hadn't known how popular she might be and had worried about just that kind of association. I *was* an idiot and not a very nice one.

We had settled into our own circles by now and they didn't overlap much. I was a grade above Amy, and we shared no classes. We didn't even share lunch periods.

One thing we did share was a friend. Tiffany and I might never have said a word to each other if it hadn't been for Amy.

~

"Hey, Martin." I looked up. It was Marlon. "We've got to talk."

"Now? We only have a minute."

"Um, no. Lunch time would be better."

I nodded. It was just before second period, math, on Tuesday, and I hadn't seen Marlon since the festival. He usually found a ride to school, rather than take the bus. I wondered, briefly, what was on his mind but then I had to concentrate on algebra.

I've mentioned my misgivings about Marlon and his friends. Still, I sat with them at lunch, not taking part in the conversation much, but adding commentary (okay, wise cracks) at times. It was pretty much the role I had always assumed.

Today, Marlon sat down opposite me. His tray, as usual, was overflowing.

"How do you stay so thin?" I asked. "You eat like a horse and a pig combined." He probably heard that kind of thing too often.

Marlon shoved back his mop of hair. It was dark and curly, like his sister's. "Say," he began, "I hope I didn't come off bigoted or something with the stuff I said on Saturday. I mean, you don't think I'm a complete ass, do you?"

"Because you think Frank Hanley is 'white trash?'" I figured I might as well be frank. Well, Frank is actually frank but you know what I mean.

That certainly derailed Marlon's train of thought. He leaned back, holding a spoon of mashed potatoes. With catsup; yuck!

"Yeah," he said, "I guess that's about it."

He recovered and started eating again. "I know Frank has it hard at home. I've watched him and his dysfunctional family (Marlon actually used words like that) all my life. Maybe he's not really a bad kid but he has been in trouble a couple of times."

I gave him a questioning look.

"Oh, just minor vandalism. Him and some of the guys he used to run around with. I guess Dell has been a good influence on him."

"Well, I hope I am, too." I was half-serious.

"Uh-huh. And you live a lot closer so he has someone to hang with after school. Someone without a record—uh, you are clean, aren't you?" he cracked.

37

"That's between me and the Atlanta Police Department."

Marlon continued. "Anyway, he might do all right."

"Hope so," I said. "I'm not sure about his little brother, though." We both laughed; Jason was a ten year old terror. I wondered if Frank had been like that.

"But you know why I was concerned," Marlon went on. "Look at her, over there."

He nodded toward his sister, sitting by herself at the end of a table. She and Amy ate at different lunch periods and she had no other close friends.

In a way, Tiffany was going through something similar to me, trying to fit into a new environment. Academically, she was miles ahead of Amy. Back in Ruby, that hadn't mattered so much; now the two were starting to follow different paths.

"Tiff's been moody, lately, even more than usual. Maybe, it's all the changes, what with going to high school." He looked at me. "I don't want her picking up with the wrong people. She seems too vulnerable. You ought to understand. You're a lot alike."

That surprised me and I guess it showed.

"Well, you are. You're both that antisocial, artsy type."

I started to protest but, hey, he was probably right.

~

Band was right after lunch. That's why Tiffany ate at the same time I did. She had signed up for band, too, and was in the beginners group with me.

We, the novices, made up a third of the class, and had various levels of ability. I was picking up flute pretty quickly. I already knew one instrument and Rita had emphasized sight reading. Some guitar teachers don't think it's important. The flute had been around, anyway, and I'd messed with it some, before.

Tiffany, though, was struggling. She had a quality, old, wooden clarinet, not one of those plastic jobs. Her mom had played it when *she* was in band. Marlon having preferred percussion, the clarinet went to Tiff. She might not have chosen it on her own.

Maybe, she was feeling some resentment and transferring it to the instrument. I wouldn't have been surprised if she'd thrown it across the room in frustration. Perhaps she did, at home.

On the other hand, it could have been a strong streak of perfectionism in her. I know how that can go—I've crumpled enough drawings that failed to measure up. The fact that it was such a fine instrument and her mom's, to boot, would make it all the worse. She *had* to be good.

Mr. Montero, our music teacher, already saw me as a future marching band member. That was the old "counting your chickens" bit. I wasn't sure I wanted to invest the time, especially, all those Friday nights at games. I'd stick to the "sit-down" band for now, thank you. We only gave a couple of concerts each semester.

I asked Marlon why he went for the marching band. That meant two band classes a day for him. Marching band met during the last period and often practiced into the after-school hours, which was a definite pain. And those cheesy uniforms! Someone had opted for "Aussie" hats.

"Most of my friends are in the band," he replied, "and we enjoy doing things together. You may not care about that but I'm hardly the hermit type. Could help me get a scholarship, too, if I become a music major."

Marlon wasn't sure about a career but he did know where he wanted to go to school. There were University of Florida "Gator" stickers plastered on all his belongings.

"Besides," Marlon pointed out, "there just aren't enough other interesting classes available."

~

I was in the restaurant, doing homework on one of the tables. Over at the counter, Mom was putting together table settings. I looked up and asked her something I'd thought about from time to time. It seemed more relevant, now.

"How do you and Dad get along so well?" They did, too, though they had occasional disagreements, like everyone. "You're so different."

"Opposites attract?"

"But birds of a feather flock together," came Dad's voice from the kitchen.

"And early to bed and early to rise makes for a boring life. Enough with the adages," I said.

"I don't think we're all that different. Do you?" Mom called to Dad.

"Different temperaments," he said, coming into the room, "but similar interests."

"Yes. Our personalities compliment each other. That's what makes a good team." Mom had a tendency to think in terms of management clichés. "I suppose each of us makes up for the other's weaknesses."

"Not that I have any," maintained Dad.

"I can think of a few," she shot back, "but we're compatible, anyway."

"That means she digs me." Dad hugged her.

Okay, I thought. My parents do like a lot of the same things and share pretty much the same values. That certainly helps. If they didn't, they'd still be back in Atlanta. Or one of them would.

I knew Mom was sometimes irritated by Dad's laid back attitude. Just as often, her approach seemed overly aggressive to Dad. But the fact that they could come to decisions together kept either one from becoming resentful.

Perhaps that was it. You could be very different but if you shared enough interests, if you reached for the same items on life's shelf, it could work. But I knew relationships might be a tad more complicated than that.

Chapter 9

A few days later, we were in the restaurant again, just before dinner. I sat at a table with Frank, helping him with his homework.

"We need to find someone to work in the restaurant on weekend mornings," my mom said to me. "I was thinking of asking Amy Akin."

"Why not Frank?" I countered. He looked up from his book. "He's around all the time, anyway." I grinned at him.

Dad stepped right into it. "Would you like to make some money, Frank?" Mom looked more than just a little peeved. She'd lost control here.

"New guitar, man," I whispered to him. I knew how to motivate Frank.

"Sure," he said. "Whatever."

"Stay for dinner?" I asked.

After Frank went home, Mom did not hesitate to share her misgivings.

"I was thinking in terms of a polite, sensible girl to waitress for me. Someone I could trust while I'm in the kitchen. I'm not sure Frank can handle that."

"You sound a bit sexist, dear."

"Oh, you know Frank lacks social skills."

"At least, he could bus and fill coffee cups and that sort of thing," I said, "and wash those dirty dishes you dread so much."

"I could let you do that." Actually, I did bus, some, but was usually "doing up" rooms when dish-washing time came.

My dad became thoughtful. "Maybe we're looking at this backwards. It might be more practical if you stayed in the front and someone else cooked."

He didn't say it outright but we all knew Mom didn't have the "right stuff" when it came to cooking. In fact, Dad and I were both more into it than she, and Jeff had held down the kitchen while he was here. "Jeff the Chef" we called him.

"We'll give Frank a try and hope it sorts out. But remember," she told Dad, "you're the one who offered him the job. If it doesn't work, you're the one who fires him."

Not that Dad could ever do that. If necessary, he'd find some other job around here for the kid.

~

Many people would be bored silly living in Ruby. Even Dad couldn't think about fishing *all* the time. But if you needed a shot of big city, it was a long drive to Orlando or Tampa. An alternative did exist in Gainesville. Although much smaller, it was a university town so all the cultural stuff was there. That was important to my folks. It was much closer, too.

My point is that you had to find your own entertainment in Ruby. So, one slow September afternoon, with no homework, no company and no ambition to practice an instrument, I hopped on the ten-speed and went looking for Mr. Edwards' studio.

Addresses around here are vague, since we have no street numbers. Usually, it's a street name and then "next to such-and-such" or "across from so-and-so." His studio was "just west of the bridge" and a "block from Riverside Road." That meant a block south, of course; north would be in the river. The main thoroughfare, Riverside Road, didn't end at the bridge. It continued to follow the river on past Parker's Restaurant and then turned south along the coast. Eventually, it curved back east to become a roundabout way to Nelson. It was longer but folks from Ruby often used this "scenic" route.

A number of "cottage industry" businesses were located near the bridge, often in old houses. This was a part of town a tourist might think "quaint" or, at least, picturesque. Small notices along the road directed one to gift shop, bed and breakfast, antiques, outboard motor repair.

One palette-shaped sign pointed me toward Edwards' studio. I turned and biked back a block, coming to a house and outlying buildings. There was no "cracker" architecture here. This was the "modern" Florida stuff: concrete-block ranch house and not a tin roof in sight. A garage-sized structure was labeled "Studio."

I walked up to its entrance, not intending to stay if Mr. Edwards was busy with customers. The sign on the door said "come in" but the place was empty.

There was a back door, hanging partly open. Maybe he'd only stepped out for a minute. I'd just take advantage of this opportunity to look the studio over while I waited.

A place like this was a dream. It had loads of room to spread out, a big easel, worktable, walls covered with paintings. In one corner was a desk and a coffee maker. It even had a sink and, I discovered later, a rest room. You could stay in this studio all day and really get some work done.

I had heard a clanking from outside. Now, I caught a voice, as well. I went to the back door and looked out. Mr. Edwards and some kid were lifting weights.

They were in a covered patio built onto the back of the studio, screened to keep out sand gnats and mosquitoes. Along with some lawn furniture were benches and a squat rack. The artist noticed me as I came to the door.

"Oh, hi—man." He remembered me but not my name. "Come to see the studio?"

"Yes, sir," I replied. "It's great."

He smiled. "Glad you like it." He waved an arm toward the boy. "You know J.R.?"

"Uh-huh. Sort of." I knew he was called J.R. I also knew he was an Akin. I didn't know whether he lived in Ruby or Blessed or somewhere in-between—that family is all over the area. "We're in the same English class."

"Yeah," he said. "You're Martin, right?"

I nodded. Mr. Edwards nodded too. He had my name, now, and it had jogged his memory.

"Well, just so we have the record straight, J.R., this is Martin Groves, budding artist, from the Hilltop Lodge." Someone must have filled him in on me. "Martin, this is Fred Akin, Junior, budding bodybuilder and better known as J.R."

"Fred Akin?" I asked. "Like the minister?"

"Pastor Fred's my father."

"It must suck to be the minister's son," joked Mr. Edwards. "We Catholics don't run into that situation."

"Mr. Edwards!" J.R. pretended to be shocked. "You shouldn't use language like that around me."

"What, suck? Nothing wrong with that word. Actually," he explained, "It's one of those expressions that came out of surfing way back in the Sixties, like 'radical' and 'gnarly.' It referred to a kind of surf condition; when the tide got so low that the waves couldn't be ridden, they'd say the surf had 'sucked out.' Got applied to any unpleasant situation, eventually."

"He's full of useless information," J.R. told me.

"All knowledge is useful," maintained Mr. Edwards. "Ready for another set?"

~

Robby knew J.R. real well. I suppose all the local kids did. I simply hadn't run into him much because he didn't ride the bus. He had older friends who would give him a lift to school.

"His uncle—you know, Amy's father—is a buddy of my dad. They go hunting and fishing together."

"I've never met Amy's dad," I said. "What's he do?"

"As little as possible. No, that's unfair, but he's *not* very ambitious. Used to be a commercial fisherman, before the net ban. Now, he's sort of a handy man."

Robby looked up as another passenger boarded the bus. Then he went on. "He started the course to get his captain's license but I guess it was too hard or something."

"My dad's taking that class."

"Yeah, well he shouldn't have any trouble. Shoot, most guys don't. Your dad fixing to be a guide?"

"Uh-huh." I'd lost interest in talking. All this had made me

45

think that things might be pretty tight for Amy and her family. Maybe, I should have encouraged Mom when she mentioned the idea of hiring her.

And I told my folks so, that evening.

Chapter 10

You might think I was too old for tree houses, but space was pretty tight in the apartment and a huge live oak grew behind the motel, so why not? There was even enough scrap lumber around to complete a platform and a ladder. Later, I figured, I'd add to it.

It was a place I could go after school to play the guitar or just find some privacy. My view of the river was great, over the roof of the Lodge. I did a load of sketches and watercolors up there.

Sometimes, Frank would haul his guitar up. With his tiny, battery-powered amp, the lack of electricity was no problem. He was improving very quickly but then it was the only thing he thought about. His enthusiasm did not extend to theory. Frank just couldn't see any reason to bother with it. I repeated what Rita had told me: "You can't break the rules if you don't know what they are."

On a Friday afternoon, Robby had ridden the bus to the Lodge with me. We sat in the oak, at sunset, Frank, Robby, and I, watching for his ride home.

"You guys going to the race on Sunday?" inquired Rob.

"Is Donny running?" Frank asked, putting down his guitar. He'd been absent-mindedly picking some riff.

"Yep. He's gonna race his new buggy. First time."

I had no clue what they were talking about and said so.

"Mud bogging, man. There's a track just north of Blessed."

"They're starting their new season."

"Every other Sunday afternoon."

"Okay, mud bogging." I nodded. "What's mud bogging?"

"It's racing on a mud track," said Robby. "You know what a dune buggy's like?"

"Yeah."

"Well, these are mud buggies. Guys around here build 'em and race 'em."

"His Uncle Donny races."

"He's been waiting all summer to try out his new buggy."

This whole mud bogging concept didn't do much for me but

my friends seemed enthusiastic. I've told you it can get awfully boring in Ruby.

"If you want to go, my dad can take us," offered Rob, "if you don't mind riding in the back of a pickup."

~

My folks said okay. By Sunday afternoon, things slow down enough at the motel that I'm not really needed. 'Most everyone checks out and hardly anyone checks in, so all the rooms don't need to be cleaned right away.

Rob called on Saturday to check whether we were going. I asked what it cost; it wasn't much so I said all right, count Frank and me in.

Dad pointed out that he expected to have his captain's papers soon. He might not be around on many of the weekends and some of the weekdays, as well.

"You'll have to take up the slack. You and your assistant." Meaning Frank. "It probably won't be an issue until the beginning of next year. Even then, I understand things are slow in January and February."

Frank had started helping in the restaurant and Mom had been right: he wasn't particularly suited to it. There was no problem if someone pointed him in the right direction but he needed more supervision than we sometimes could give. Frank was a help to Mom when it came to cleaning up. He was hopeless at waiting tables.

All of this was on weekends, of course. School mornings, Mom and Dad were on their own.

"The two of you might handle some of the outside work," said Mom. "If nothing else, I'm sure Frank could help keep an eye on the docks."

"And you're still thinking of hiring Amy?" I asked. I knew my Mom.

"I've already mentioned it to her mother."

~

Robby Dell and I didn't have a great deal in common. We got along okay, sure, but two guys like us normally wouldn't have spent much time together. When he came to the Hilltop, it was really to hang out with Frank. It was a more convenient place than either of their homes.

I've sometimes wondered if Robby resented me a bit. I was spending more time with his best friend than he was, outside of school. There, they were buddies the way they'd always been; they'd landed in many of the same classes.

But they might have been moving in different directions, anyway. That happens a lot, it seems, at our age. I could see it with Amy and Tiffany. You play with some little kid for years and then, one day, find that you no longer share the same interests.

Some of this was in my mind as we rode along in Mr. Dell's truck, our backs to the cab. Some of it, I've thought through since. It wasn't lost on me that Frank sat between us. What Rob and I did share was something of a protective, big-brotherly attitude toward our friend. We were alike in that respect.

Mud bogging demonstrated our differences. Sitting on a hard, dirty bleacher, having my hearing destroyed, was not my idea of fun. I couldn't tell one buggy from another, anyway, much less the different classes and other nuances of bogging.

Donny rode up front with Mr. Dell, his brother-in-law. He appeared to be in his mid-twenties, stocky and sandy-haired, like Robby, except with a beard. Behind the truck, on a trailer, was his buggy. It did have an interesting look to it, like one of those futur-istic war-machines boys will doodle. I'll bet Donny's notebooks had been full of them.

An open field served as a pit area. Rob and his dad helped Donny unload and prepare for the race. I figured I could help best by staying out of the way but Frank was underfoot.

"Why don't you boys go find some seats?" said Mr. Dell. He

may have been addressing all of us but he looked straight at Robby. "I'm staying down here with Don."

"Can't I help?" asked Robby.

"No, son, we can handle it. And you have guests." He looked down at us; Mr. Dell was a big guy. "You can all see better from the stands."

He reached into his back pocket for his wallet. It was attached to his belt by a chain. "Here, this should get you in and buy something to munch." He handed Rob some bills.

"Okay," said Robby, with only a hint of disappointment in his voice. "Thanks. Good luck, Uncle Donny!"

Donny gave a wave without looking up from whatever he was doing to the engine.

I never saw Rob argue with his father. He always seemed solid and even-tempered. Maybe it was his upbringing, maybe it was his nature. I don't know.

I'd brought my own cash but if Mr. Dell wanted to treat, that was fine with me. It didn't cost much, anyway. But, of we three boys, I probably had the most money. Rob received some kind of allowance but I got paid for working at the Lodge. My folks thought it made better sense than an allowance; the more I did, the more I made. That applied only to motel work, naturally. I was expected to do family chores for nothing.

"After all," reasoned Mom, "if we didn't have you around, we'd have to hire someone." They probably would have paid him more, too.

I figured I might spring for some sodas or something, later. Not too much, though. A peer's money is very different from that spent by someone's parent and the last thing Frank needed was another dose of inferiority.

There were plenty of seats. Robby steered us toward a section where families had settled in, away from the knots of beer-drinking guys.

He had experience at these events.

Chapter 11

Mud buggies are loud; really loud. They look dangerous, too. The ambulance parked by the gates definitely added to that impression but no one got hurt, this time. Machines did roll over and lots of them went sliding off the track and banging into things. Robby said the drivers weren't always so lucky.

"Has anyone got, you know, killed?" Frank asked.

"Not that I've heard of," replied Rob, "but arms and legs get busted."

I changed the subject. "When's your uncle going to run?" We'd seen five races, so far.

"Soon, I think. There are two preliminary heats in his class."

I spotted Donny's garish green and orange vehicle moving toward the starting line. "Here he comes," I announced.

"Yeah! Go, Donny!" yelled Frank.

"Shee. Can't you wait till they start?" I kidded.

"He can't hear me then," laughed Frank.

"He can't hear you anytime," Robby pointed out.

Donny lined up with three other machines. I could tell him not only by his color scheme but by the "Don Steiner" shakily lettered on the side. Half-way through the first muddy lap and they'd all look the same, at least to me.

Then they were off and sliding around the track for ten laps, or was it twelve? Frank and Robby were on their feet for the entire race. I always feel sort of silly cheering but "when in Rome," so I stood up too.

Winning seemed to require luck as much as driving skill. The buggies, themselves, were pretty evenly matched. As long as something didn't break, one was as good as another.

At the end of the race, Frank and Robby were both cheering: "Yeah! Way to go!"

"Did I miss something?" I asked. "Didn't Donny lose?"

"He came in second," explained Robby. "He'll advance to the final."

"Oh. Want something to drink?"

~

I could see Rob's uncle and father huddled over the buggy, next to Mr. Dell's big pickup truck. They were doing whatever mechanic types do.

Mr. Dell saw me, too, and ambled over. He was tall and probably had been thin when he was younger. Now he had a pretty good pot. His black hair was going too but he kept it covered up with a cap.

He greeted me through the chain-link fence and asked if we were enjoying ourselves.

"We don't meet many of Robby's school friends," he said, "living out in the country like we do."

"It is too far away by bike, sir," I replied. That's me: always polite. "But," I continued (don't ask me why), "next year I'll be driving."

"Oh. Then you're Robby's age? Didn't know that." He stood there a moment, wiping his hands with an oily rag, while it sank in. "I figured you for someone in his class, like Frank."

What could I say to that? I know I'm smallish.

"Well, that's good, I reckon. He needs friends his own age. Hope to see more of you, son."

He headed back to the buggy, leaving me to wonder, "What was that all about?"

Robby may never have said much to his folks about me. We were very different; perhaps, he didn't know what to say. Mr. Dell could have been trying to check me out, find out who I was without being blatant about it.

~

By the time I returned, they'd finished the second preliminary in Donny's division. The final would be sometime later. We sat in the afternoon sun and sipped our lemonades. It was still quite warm. Back in Atlanta, they were starting to feel the fall weather but nothing had penetrated this far south.

I mentioned it to the guys.

"We ought to get a bit cooler soon, shouldn't we?" Frank asked Rob.

"I think so," he replied. "Some fronts make it through by October."

Frank turned to me. "You have cable. You'll know before us."

"Those winter storms can really hit hard. As hard as a hurricane," said Robby.

A hurricane had blown by, a hundred miles out in the Gulf, in late August. All it had done was bring down some branches and make the tides a little higher than normal.

At last, Donny's race came up. He finished third but no one seemed to care.

~

"They're just a bunch of 'good ol' boys' having fun," said Rob. "Someone different wins every time."

"Do you go a lot?" I asked him.

"Naw. Donny and my dad are into it more than me."

"I like it," Frank commented.

"We noticed," I said. "So, what do you do, instead?"

"I'd rather fish. Or hunt—the season starts soon. In fact," he continued, bashfully, like he was letting some big secret out, "I think I'd like to be a charter-boat captain some day. Like your dad's fixing to do."

"There's a great choice for career day."

"Yeah. Dad wants me to learn a trade, like welding."

"You could be a small-engine mechanic," suggested Frank. "Outboard motors always seem to need work."

"If you're good at mechanical stuff," I added. "I'm Mr. Badwrench, myself."

"I don't really enjoy it, like my uncle."

The truck slowed down. We were about to turn off Nineteen, toward Ruby.

"What about gun-smithing?" I'd always thought that sounded like a neat occupation.

Robby laughed. "Most people would see that as a hobby, not a job."

"Like fishing," Frank pointed out.

Donny had opened the cab's rear window. "We're going to stop and unload the buggy, first. That any problem for you guys?"

"Not for me," I answered. "How 'bout you, Frank?" He shook his head.

"You could, um, stay for dinner," Robby suggested, kind of shyly. I wasn't sure whether he really wanted us or was just being polite.

It didn't matter. "Great," enthused Frank. "Is your mom fixing fried chicken?"

"She *always* fries chicken on Sundays."

"I'd have to call my folks," I warned, but I knew they'd say okay.

~

"They do say grace," Frank whispered to me.

I'd expected that; they probably bowed their heads, too. My parents don't when they pray. Mom says that humility doesn't require "groveling," but I'm sure the Dells just saw it as being respectful.

Not being inclined to rock the boat, I bowed my head with the rest of them. A little.

It was a big table and a big family. Donny and his wife and their two toddlers were there. Robby's grandfather sat at one end of the table; friends and relatives filled the other chairs. I met Rob's little sister, Rita Marie, who'd just started kindergarten. I told her I knew a Rita but she wasn't impressed.

How many of these people actually lived there, I'm not sure. Two trailers stood near the Dell's home. I knew the Steiners occupied one.

Mr. and Mrs. Dell tried to take the opportunity to grill me for information. Too much was going on, though, too many distractions, and I'm not inclined to volunteer a lot. I probably left a reasonably good impression: a nice boy, polite but dull. I don't believe they saw me as stand-offish, though Mrs. Dell didn't think I ate enough of her chicken.

After our thanks and goodbyes, Mr. Dell drove Frank and me back to the Lodge. We got to ride in the cab, this time, and were all too mellow to talk much. It's only a ten minute drive, anyway.

Frank pedaled his bike off into the dark and I went straight to bed: tomorrow was a school day. It took a while to fall asleep.

Chapter 12

"My parents like you. They think I should hang around more with 'mature' guys." Robby made the "quotes" sign with his fingers.

"If only they knew," snickered Frank.

"They were probably comparing me to you," I retorted.

Robby said, kind of softly, "They *were* comparing you to Frank," and let that sink in. He really should have kept his mouth shut but I guess it bothered him.

"The hell with them," said Frank.

"Watch your mouth, Mr. Hanley," came the bus driver's voice. "I don't want to write you a referral."

"The hell with you, too," he blurted out. He said nothing else, all the way to school.

Frank stayed in his seat while everyone else disembarked. We waited for him, just outside.

"I'm sorry," said Frank. "I didn't mean to say that to you."

"I know," sighed Mrs. Cannon. "I hear more of what goes on in this bus than you might think. But you know," she continued, "I could write you up. I'm *supposed* to write you up. Now move along; I need some coffee." She looked down at Rob and me. "Try to keep him out of trouble."

We felt like his parents.

~

Amy came over one evening, later that week, to help her mom clean fish. The fishing was picking up and should be good until the end of the year. I filled Amy in on the incident with Frank. It wasn't gossip; she was a friend and ought to know.

She and her mother were at the fish cleaning station. Mrs. Akin would slice the fillets off, pass them to Amy, and chuck the carcasses into the water. The catfish and crabs loved that. Amy would wash the pieces and pack them in plastic bags.

I leaned on the end of the counter. "What's everyone got against Frank?" I asked. "They all seem to have it in for him."

"Mrs. Cannon doesn't. I'd say she likes Frank," replied Amy.

"Yeah, she seemed concerned about him."

"She knew his father," Betty Akin said. We turned to look at her. "And she was a friend of his grandmother."

"She's dead," Amy informed me.

"His father might as well be. No one's heard from him in years." Mrs. Akin started in on another fish. She glanced up to see that we were still looking at her. "You're not getting any more details from me. The whole thing's too sordid for adults, much less you two." She swatted a mosquito. "Turn the fan up, will you?"

~

My folks sympathized with Frank but weren't much help. My dad did make one suggestion.

"Why don't you invite Frank and Robby over to go fishing, sometime? I could use the practical experience. Getting my license is only half the job."

"Make it this weekend," said Mom. "We'll be too busy the next, with the three day holiday." She paused. "I'm going to give Amy a try then."

"What kind of people would stay for Columbus Day?" I asked. "I mean, only kids and postal workers get it off, right?"

"And bankers and teachers," added Dad. "We were always able to take a little vacation."

"Maybe it's bankers taking their kids fishing," I suggested. "I'll invite Robby and Frank tomorrow. Is Saturday or Sunday better?"

"It don't make no never mind." Dad was starting to sound like a local.

~

"Are you going to wear a cute little waitress uniform?" Rob asked.

"Naw, man, that would scare the customers away," said Frank.

Amy looked scornfully from one to the other. "I'll bet they

liked it when *you* were there. Did the old ladies pinch your cheeks?" she asked Frank.

He reddened up immediately, even though he laughed with the rest of us. Frank was so easy, sometimes.

"Next year, Tiffany and I may work at Parker's Restaurant," Amy said. "There will be an opening when Messy leaves."

Tiffany gave her an odd look. I thought I knew why and brought up a different subject.

"J.R. said he saw us Sunday, at the track."

"Yeah?" Robby said. "I didn't notice him."

"I didn't know J.R. was a buddy of yours," said Amy.

"We're in the same English class and I've run into him after school." It seemed like he worked out almost every afternoon with Mr. Edwards. The last time I'd gone over, I'd tried a little lifting, myself.

"How about asking him to go fishing with us?" suggested Robby.

"Okay with me," I answered. "My dad won't mind one more." Frank didn't seem big on the idea. "That all right, man?" I asked him.

"I guess. Sure."

Robby had said "no problem" for either day but we could get an earlier start on Saturday. His family was at church most Sunday mornings. Frank had just said "whatever."

We were pulling into Blessed. I gathered up my flute and my pack. Exiting the bus, I whispered to Rob, "I'm not going to ask J.R. I think Frank wants it to be just the three of us."

"Oh. Yeah, you're probably right. Kind of late to invite him, anyway."

"Uh-huh. I might mention it some other time."

He nodded and we headed in opposite directions.

~

Sometimes I ate with Marlon and his friends; sometimes I sat down across from Tiffany. We might not talk much but that was okay. If we did, it was usually about band.

I was seated first, today, and I waved for her to join me. I wasn't sure that she would but, with only a moment's hesitation, she brought her tray over.

After a while, I said, "That job at Parker's won't be offered to Amy, will it?"

She shook her head. "Amy assumes things she shouldn't. There's only one opening."

"And you're family."

"Yes." She pushed some peas around with her fork. "I don't know if I even want the job. Amy'd be better at it."

"Maybe they'll need someone else by next year," I suggested. "I thought restaurants had a lot of turnover."

"Almost everyone there is related. It's one, big, happy, Greek family." She sounded just a tad sarcastic. "Except for Uncle Jim."

"Mr. Parker?"

"Good guess." She smiled. "He mostly sticks to cooking and lets my aunt run the place. He's the only one there who can make a decent hush-puppy."

"Isn't Marlon, um, next in line?" I wondered.

Tiffany's expression became hard to read. "Mom and Dad think it's better for him to be active in school. I mean, rather than hold down a job."

Of course, Tiff wasn't active in much of anything. I wondered if her folks gave her a hard time about it; mine were forever urging me to be more outgoing.

Chapter 13

"Cold weather brings trout into the river," stated Robby. "That's what a lot of fishermen come for."

He was talking about the "speckled sea trout," a fish unrelated to the trout in freshwater streams. "We might find a few but it's really too early in the season."

"True," said Dad. "I figured our best bet was to head offshore."

"If nothing else, we might hook some black bass."

If ever two kindred spirits existed, they were Robby Dell and David Groves. They were the fishermen here. Frank and I were just along for the ride.

"I'm glad we didn't bring Jason," Frank whispered to me. His mom had tried to saddle him with his little brother but he would have nothing to do with it. The situation wasn't helped any when her boyfriend decided to add his input. Frank loved his mom, of course, but not the guy she was living with.

I was afraid Frank's day would be canceled before it started. Fortunately, Jason didn't want to be with him any more than he wanted to be with Jason. So, finally, they let him out of the car with his fishing tackle and drove off. The rest of us had been sitting on the dock, trying to act like we weren't listening.

It took less time to get down the river than the last trip I'd made. The big Yamaha outboard really pushed us along.

Frank noted the motor's manufacturer. "They make basses, too," he said. "Maybe you'd like one of them." He hadn't given up on that idea.

"How 'bout in 'sea foam green?'" I asked.

"Yuck!" Frank didn't go for "retro" colors. "Why would anyone want a pastel axe?"

"Oh, you don't think it's macho enough unless it's black."

"Dark blue's okay."

~

The light southerly wind indicated an approaching cold front. It was really a nice day to be out on the water.

We fished some, we ate and drank, we listened to the radio. I found that, out in the Gulf, I could pick up stations way up in the Panhandle.

We caught black drum, which aren't much good to eat, and we caught red drum, a.k.a. red fish, which are. But we threw them both back. Dad and Robby were very much into the "catch and release" philosophy. Then we anchored at a spot where black bass were reputed to be thick.

Those little guys are fun—and easy—to catch. Amy tells me they taste good but are a pain to clean. It didn't matter; we released them, too.

The sky grew overcast. First thing in the morning, there had only been a few high clouds scudding by. Now they were getting thicker and lower.

Dad looked up. "That winter weather's going to roll in soon."

"The TV said rain tonight and maybe in the morning," I said. "Then a little cooler. Not exactly winter."

"I guess it's never all that wintry here."

"I saw snow, once," reported Frank. "Remember, Robby?"

"Yeah, two years ago. Just a few flakes."

"Was it really cold?" I asked.

"Down around twenty, I think," answered Robby. "But we may drop that low a couple times during the winter."

"I thought this tropical Florida," joked Dad.

"Just wait until a big winter storm brings the river up into your front yard," Robby warned us.

~

We headed in by mid-afternoon. The wind was picking up some, by then, and getting more westerly. We knew the rain would be along, soon.

"Here's the river," announced Frank, as we slid by a channel marker.

Dad began making a long arc to the East.

61

"I see Messy's car," called Frank, from the bow. He was scanning the shoreline with binoculars.

"She's always at the restaurant at this time," Rob replied.

"Uh-huh," Frank absently answered. He was more interested in ogling Melissa's Mustang. "You like that dark red?"

"It's okay," I said, "but if they start giving them away, I'll take blue."

"Not sea foam green?" kidded Frank. "You're making money. You could get a car next year."

"Not a brand-new Mustang. Messy makes more than the three of us combined."

"She works harder than the three of us combined," Robby observed.

"Ah, yes," commented my dad, "there's nothing like a woman with a steady job."

"Right," Frank agreed. "We'll just have to hang around with Amy when she starts working at Parker's."

"Um, yeah." I wasn't going to get into that.

We passed under the bridge. Dad had to slow down some; he didn't want to put out a big wake where other boats were on the river.

We'd be home in twenty minutes.

~

"I'd say that was a success," my dad told my mom. "Did you have any trouble here?"

She kissed him. "No. It was a little hectic, early." She stepped back. "If you start taking parties out on a regular basis, some help around here is going to be very welcome."

Frank and Robby stowed their gear in our new SUV. Dad had insisted that we needed a four-wheel drive to get boats up and down the launching ramp.

"It's not that late," I said. "You want to hang around a while?" It was about the time we'd normally get home from school. "Maybe you could stay for dinner."

Frank sniffed the air. "We smell kinda bad."

"Yeah," admitted Rob. "We'd better go home and clean up.

"I'll be over tomorrow," said Frank.

Chapter 14

A heavy squall line passed through around midnight. It was still drizzling when I awoke.

We waited for Frank to come help with breakfast but he never showed. My folks thought something like this was to be expected. I didn't.

At about nine, a worn compact pulled up out front. Frank's mom came in and walked straight back to the counter where I was talking to my mother. I knew they hadn't met before.

"Mom, this is Ms. Differs." That didn't ring a bell with her. "Frank's mother." Differs was the name of her second husband, Jason's father.

"Oh—how do you do?"

"Mrs. Groves, Martin, has Frank been here?" She seemed nearly in tears. "Do you know where he is?"

"We haven't heard from him."

"We thought he'd be here this morning," I added.

"There was a terrible fight with Bill last night. He never slept in his bed." She lit up a cigarette, despite the "no smoking" signs. Mom didn't stop her. "I don't know what's wrong with that boy."

Mom poured a cup of coffee and handed it to her. I knew her well enough to push the artificial sweetener her way.

My mother turned to me. "Do you have any ideas?"

I shook my head. "I don't think he would have stayed out in that weather."

Ms. Differs looked for a place to deposit her ash. Mom set a saucer down. "Use this," she said. That must have really hurt.

Julie Differs was younger than my parents, in her mid-thirties. She was just a teenager when Frank was born.

A lot of guys thought she was attractive, too: very thin, very blonde. She had the whole "waif" thing going. Shoot, even I thought she was sexy.

A horn honked outside. "That's Bill. We're going to check some other places. Please, please, call if you hear anything at all."

"Have you notified the police?" asked Mom.

"No, not yet."

"The sooner, the better," said my mother. "If he really wanted, Frank could be a long way from here by now."

Ms. Differs nodded and left.

I looked at my mom. "Can I go check something out? It'll only take a minute or two."

"Go ahead. I think I can handle this." She waved her arm at the nearly empty restaurant. One old man was sitting in a corner, drinking coffee and reading the paper.

Where would Frank have gone to avoid the storm last night? One possibility was in my own back yard. I had the tree house partially enclosed now. It might not be weather-tight but it was shelter.

Frank wasn't there (I'd hoped he might be) but he'd left a friend. "PLEASE KEEP FOR ME" said the sign taped to his guitar. That was the only message. He probably didn't know where he was going, anyway.

I told my folks about it and they called Frank's mother.

~

A big green-and-white from the Sheriff's office pulled up around noon. I don't know why the law persists in driving those tanks.

The deputy who stepped out matched up pretty well with his vehicle. He was big, in every direction, and looked young.

"Mrs. Groves? How do you do? I'm Deputy Ortiz. And you're Martin?"

"Yes, sir."

"All right. As you no doubt guessed, I'm here about the Hanley boy. Frank." My dad had walked up from the docks.

"This is Mr. Groves," said my mom. "Would you like to come in and sit down?"

"I'd appreciate it, ma'am."

The deputy asked his questions: When did we last see Frank? Did we have any idea where he might go? That kind of thing.

"Now you think he stopped here last night. Did any of you see him?"

We all shook our heads.

"I think he might have slept awhile," I said. He'd used the blanket I had up there.

"Okay. This is some kind of shed around back?"

"No, sir, it's a tree house."

"Oh. Let's take a look."

Dad and Deputy Ortiz and I went around to the oak.

"He left his guitar and a note. Do you want me to go get them?"

"No need," he answered and went right up the ladder. He may have been big, and kind of fat, but he had no problem. I hoped my construction was up to snuff; Deputy Ortiz looked like he would land pretty hard.

I followed him up. He looked the place over, read the note, and said, "Not much here."

He turned to me. "You get up early?"

I nodded. "Five."

"If he didn't want to be seen, he would have left before then." He shrugged. "Not that that is any help." He ran his fingers through his short, dark hair. "You know about his problems at home."

It was a statement more than a question.

"Yes, sir."

"Do you know if Bill Watson ever hit him?" He paused. "Or anyone else in that household?"

"He—never said so."

"But you aren't sure."

"No." I did know that Frank's mother and Bill got into some heavy arguments at times. The neighbors had even called for a deputy, once. Of course, this guy would be aware of that.

Ortiz didn't look quite as agile going down the ladder as he had going up. On the ground, he thanked Dad and me for our time.

"I haven't seen you here, before," said Dad. "It's always been Deputy White or Deputy Grimes." Both stopped occasionally.

"No, sir, I don't normally serve the area. It's not even my county, but I requested this duty." He considered going on, and did. "I've known Julie Differs a long time. Went to school with her."

~

No more news came, neither Sunday afternoon nor Monday morning. Many of the kids at school had heard about it and I was called on to supply details.

Then, Monday afternoon, Mrs. Cannon put her hand on my arm as I boarded the bus.

"Frank's okay," she said. "They picked him up outside of Gainesville."

I slid into the front seat. Robby got on and I patted the seat beside me. "Man, they found Frank."

"Is he all right?"

"He's fine," said Mrs. Cannon. "Just tired and hungry."

We must have both given her questioning looks.

"I have my sources." She smiled. "Well, Mrs. Ortiz, actually."

"The deputy's wife?" I asked.

"His mother," she answered. "Buddy's not married."

"I know Mrs. Ortiz," said Rob. "She works at the Piggly-Wiggly. She's the manager."

"Oh, the old woman with the accent?"

Mrs. Cannon laughed. "She's not any older than I am." She shut the doors and prepared to pull out.

"Sorry," I said, "you just look so much younger." Good recovery, Martin.

Robby asked "Do you know what they'll do with Frank?"

"Keep him in custody a little while and then give him back to

67

his mother, I reckon." The line of busses began moving. "Not that doing that will fix anything."

~

Mom and Dad knew. Deputy Ortiz had been by with the news. He was going to bring Frank home in the morning.

There was definitely a conspiracy going on and my parents wouldn't let me in on it. "You'll know if it works out," my dad said, but Mom relented, a bit.

"We don't need to be quite that secretive. I intend to talk to Ms. Differs in the morning. After that Watson man has left. What does he do, dear?"

"Construction work of some kind. They always start early."

"Yes. Julie said he'd be gone, anyway."

"You've been talking with Frank's mom?" I asked.

"We spent some time on the phone, this afternoon. After the good news came." She collected her thoughts. "Frank won't arrive before ten."

"Can I stay home?"

"No." In stereo.

What could Mom want with Ms. Differs? Would she give her motherly advice? I'd heard her say before that someone "needed a good talking to" but I'd never known her to actually do it.

Chapter 15

"Guess what?" said Frank.

"You've been grounded until you're thirty? And you have a criminal record?"

He'd been waiting at the Lodge when I got off the bus.

"I'm moving in!"

"Here?"

"Yep. I already have some of my junk in your room." He amended that: "*Our* room."

We went up the drive and into the restaurant.

"Hey, Mom," I said, "look what followed me home. Can I keep it?"

"Is it house-broken?" she asked.

"No, but we can tie it up outside, for now."

Frank had gotten used to my family and didn't pay attention to this sort of thing, anymore. I went into the kitchen to find a snack. "You want anything, Frank?" I called.

"No, your mom fed me."

"So, what's the story?"

"I convinced Frank's mother that he and Bill Watson could not coexist in that house. She didn't need much convincing; she really knew it, already. And," she continued, "Deputy Ortiz backed me up. He told her she could lose Frank if there's more trouble."

"Deputy Buddy's a cool guy, " said Frank. "Did you know he played football at Pinelands High?"

"Doesn't surprise me," I said.

"And he benches three-twenty. Almost."

"He weighs that much. Almost."

"I think your mother was glad to find a solution," Mom told Frank. "Even one that had you moving out."

"She'll get over it." Frank tried to sound nonchalant.

Then he said, "I wish Bill was the one who moved out."

"So does Deputy Ortiz," I remarked. I probably should have kept my mouth shut.

"Huh?"

"It's pretty obvious that he has, uh, feelings for your mother."

"You picked up on that?" asked Mom. "I'm afraid your father missed it entirely."

"Maybe they were high school sweethearts. Until," I said to Frank, "your father came along and stole her away. He's nursed a broken heart all these years."

Frank had no clue as to whether I was serious. "He did ask a lot of questions about Mom. Especially whether Bill ever hurt her. Or me."

Mom shook her head at me but I had enough sense to avoid that subject.

"Let's see about fitting your stuff into the room. Boy, won't Jeff be surprised to find he has an extra brother."

And, I thought, so do I. I'd always wanted a little brother but Mom and Dad would never cooperate.

~

Dad took us over later to get the rest of Frank's things. He didn't hesitate to hug his mom before he left.

The next day, Mom drove Frank and me to school, leaving Dad in charge. Frank's new address and phone number and all that had to be straightened out with the office. Mrs. Differs was supposed to call but Mom likes to do her business face-to-face.

Going in the front doors, I stopped to look at the two big trophy cases flanking the office. Normally, they didn't interest me.

"Frank," I called, waving him over, "look at this."

There he was, Gustavo "Buddy" Ortiz, football hero. I'd thought I remembered seeing him.

"Hey, he has the school record for sacks," noted Frank

"I wouldn't have stood between him and the quarterback," I remarked. "He was pretty big, even then."

"Ugly, too, wasn't he?"

I'd noticed his acne-scarred face, before; he'd had a bad case. A fat, homely, pimply kid, and ethnic, to boot.

Mom had come up behind us. "Classic over-achiever," she said. That sounded awfully pat but it also sounded true.

Frank and I headed for our first period classes while Mom headed in to take care of business.

The way Mom handled this whole affair had taken me by surprise. It seemed more like something Dad might come up with but I think it surprised him, too. As a teacher, Dad had gotten used to seeing kids in trouble, kids he couldn't help; it was something new for Mom. She saw it as a problem to be solved, a deal to be worked out and a solution to be implemented.

There would be drawbacks to having Frank on board but we all knew it was the best answer. I already regretted having such a slob for a roommate and he was probably not trainable.

~

I was sitting at a lunch table with Marlon, filling him in. I waved for Tiffany to come over but she shook her head.

"She avoids me," said Marlon, "and my friends."

"I'm sure it's your friends more than you."

"Probably." He shoveled in some chili. "But she doesn't seem to mind you."

"She tolerates me."

"That's saying a lot, for Tiff. She even talks with you."

"Some," I admitted. Neither of us was that much of a conversationalist. "I'm certainly not very close to her. You know that."

"No," he said, "you're not really close until she reads you one of her poems."

He smiled at my expression. "Not much of it gets beyond the family and Amy. It's pretty awful stuff."

I smiled now. "I guess I've written my own share of bad poetry."

"You know, I'm one of the editors of *The Pine Tree*." That was a student "literary" magazine. "I've tried to get Tiff to submit something but no luck. Maybe you could encourage her. For that matter, if you have anything, let us see it." He laughed. "You know how dreadful our first number this year was. We're desperate!"

I did know. Either some of the kids didn't realize how badly they wrote or they just weren't easily embarrassed. But Tiffany was *too* easily embarrassed. So was I, really.

~

"Hey, Tiff, where's Amy? I thought she rode the bus this morning."

"Cheerleaders." She practically spat the word out.

"Yeah," said Robby. "She made the squad, somehow."

"She was a cheerleader at middle school," Frank reminded him.

"Anyone could make it in Ruby," Rob responded.

Amy was one of those girls who looks a little plump but is actually strong and athletic. She wasn't real interested in competitive sports but cheerleading fit her personality.

"How's she get home?" I asked.

"J.R.'s mom is picking them both up," said Tiffany. "Why do you care?"

I shrugged. "Just curious." She wasn't in a good mood.

Tiff buried her nose in a book the rest of the way home.

I turned to Robby. "Got any plans for Friday?" We had a "teacher planning day" coming up. "My mom's taking Frank and me shopping in Gainesville."

"Early start on Christmas?"

"Naw. Not unless something catches my eye. Hey," I said to Frank, "I guess I have to get you a gift, now that you're part of the family."

"I was going to give you something, anyway," he replied. Yeah, Frank would do that.

"Actually, we're going to check out some of the music stores. I don't know if we'll buy anything," I continued. I wasn't going to commit to purchasing a bass. "But we've both got some money saved."

Robby nodded. "Some of us are going out to do repairs on the hunting camp." A group of local guys leased a piece of swampland and had a cabin on it.

"Doesn't your dad have to work?" Frank inquired.

"Yeah, but Amy's father is driving out. He's bringing J.R., and Donny plans to take off at noon." Donny operated a little garage in Ruby and could set his own hours, within reason. "My dad will come Saturday and we'll stay the whole weekend.

On a sudden impulse, I asked, "Tiffany, you want to come along?"

She looked up. "Okay," she said and went back to her book.

Chapter 16

A quality classical guitar. A really nice, solid wood, made-in-Spain instrument. That's what I'd been saving for, always putting away part of my earnings.

What I played was a decent student model: plywood body, Taiwan-made and certainly not concert quality. I wanted something better.

It would cost, and cost plenty. I'm talking a thousand, maybe more. And I finally had enough saved, sort of; my folks had promised "matching funds." Three months of working at the Lodge had put me over the top.

I wasn't the only one making money. Frank had been helping, off and on, for a while; more since he moved in. Amy had worked two weekends now, as well.

She was good at the waitress thing. Sure, we could have gotten by without her but Amy did make it easier to handle breakfast.

Amy presented a problem to me, now. Having invited Tiffany to go shopping, should I also include her best friend? Would Tiffany even *want* Amy along?

The only thing to do was ask Tiffany.

"Don't bother," she said. "Amy's going to spend the day with her father."

"Oh?" It took me a second to get what that meant. "Oh, out at their camp."

"Right. She invited me but—" She looked slightly embarrassed. "I was glad to have an excuse not to go." Then she realized how that sounded. "Not that I just wanted an excuse. I mean, I'd like to go with—to go shopping."

"Uh-huh. My mom will be glad to have you along." I smiled. "Moral support."

Tiff smiled too. For two people who didn't say that much to each other, we communicated pretty well.

~

"Don't expect us to spend all day at music stores," warned my mom. "I want mall time."

"So do we, Mom. I've picked out three places that are easy to reach. See?" I held up a map. "One here and one right over here. And this one's close to the mall."

"Aw, man, there are lots more," complained Frank.

"Most of the others just carry specialty stuff, like organs."

"I thought you were only looking this time, anyway," said Mom.

"Maybe." Frank wasn't going to promise anything.

"We can only take in so much," I told Frank. "This'll let us catch some major brands."

"Let me see your list." Of course, I'd written down what each store carried. "Mmm. Okay. Uh-huh. Gibson? Aren't they too expensive?"

"But they sure are purty," I protested, "and looking is free." And I'd already figured we weren't likely to reach that particular store.

"When's that girl getting here? We could have picked her up, you know." Tiffany wasn't late; that's just Mom.

In fact, she arrived exactly when she said she would, eight o'clock sharp. Her father dropped her. He ran one of Ruby's seafood companies. It was called the "Ruby Seafood Company," naturally.

~

"She *hates* the clarinet."

"He's exaggerating," Tiffany told my mom.

"He does that," she replied. "But you really don't like the instrument, do you?"

"I've come to terms with it." I thought Tiffany would leave it at that but, after a pause, she added "I should have held out for drums."

Marlon's choice. She could never catch up in her sibling rivalry.

"Turn on the radio, will you?" requested Frank.

Tiffany looked at Mom, who nodded okay. It was tuned to a country station.

"You want that?" Tiffany asked us.

"Whatever you like, Tiffany," my mom replied. "You're in charge."

"Uh-oh," joked Frank.

I had no idea what kind of music Tiff went for. I'd kind of assumed country because that's what Amy liked. I just prayed it wasn't sappy pop or "boy bands."

"I hear too much of this," she said, mainly to herself, and punched another preset.

"Ooh, Springsteen," cooed Mom. I had to laugh. She loves Bruce.

"That's an oldies station," complained Frank, leaning over the front seat. "Can't you find something new?"

"Hey," I said, "I thought you were the guy who liked 'classic' rock."

"I know where to find that." Tiffany brought up a station that played a mix of new and old rock, the harder stuff. She left it there.

It's an hour and a half, maybe two hours, to Gainesville. It depends on the traffic on these winding two-lane roads. You can be stuck behind a cattle truck for a long time.

Everything should be open by the time we arrived.

~

Shiny new guitars are beautiful. Even the cheap ones. We took in one store, then another.

Of course, Mom and Tiff weren't going to sit in the wagon while Frank and I browsed. Mom checked out some of the keyboards; she'd had piano lessons as a girl and could still play a mean "Chopsticks." Tiffany seemed quietly interested in just about everything. She even patted the congas experimentally.

Frank's goal, though, was to score a "real" amp. "Twenty-five watts, at least," he said. "Anything less is useless."

A salesman had been hovering nearby. "True enough," he agreed, "for performing. Especially with transistor amps." He was young; maybe a college student at his part-time job. "With tubes, you might not need as much power."

"Tubes?" asked my mom. She had come over when she saw the sales guy descend on us. "I didn't know anything still used tubes."

Frank and I grinned. It's nice to be more knowledgeable than an adult.

"Everyone uses tubes, Mrs. Groves," explained Frank. "They sound better." He didn't know that from experience but it didn't stop him from expressing an opinion.

"There are plenty of very good sounding solid-state amps around. Some players prefer them and they are less expensive." The salesman turned to Frank. "I use one."

"Are you in a band?"

"Yep, 'The Malfunction.'" He paused to see if we recognized the name. "We're a ska band."

"We don't know any bands in Gainesville," I said. "We live over on the Gulf."

"Oh. Well, look over the amps and let me know if I can help," he told Frank. Tiffany had wandered over to join the group. "Anything else I can show you today?"

Mom looked at me. "I was just checking out classicals," I said. I didn't know whether to add to that.

But, hey, as long as I was here. "I've been sort of thinking of getting a bass." It wouldn't hurt to look, after all.

"Ever played?"

"No."

My mom broke in. "But he's been on classical guitar for four years. He's very good." Way to embarrass me, Mom.

"Ah." He took a thoughtful look at me and chose a bass. "Here's a decent mid-priced instrument. Want to try it on for size?"

I guess I hadn't realized how large a bass is. "It's awfully heavy," I said, "And the neck's so long." I'd become instantly disenchanted.

"Actually, that's one of the lighter basses here but I figured it still might be too big for you." He put it back. "I have a used instrument that may be ideal." He got on a step-stool and lifted it down from its place near the ceiling. "Especially for smaller hands."

It looked more like an over-sized violin than a bass guitar. I recognized the style and so did Mom.

"Oh," she said, "it looks just like the one Paul McCartney played."

"Who's Paul McCarthy?" Frank whispered.

"Beatles," I whispered back. He'd heard of them, I hoped.

"Yes, ma'am. Except this is a cheap Korean copy of the cheap German original. Here, see how it feels." He handed it to me.

It was pretty, even scuffed up a bit. Light, too; it felt good. I liked this one. "I've never seen this brand," I said. Be cautious, Martin.

"That model's sold under a bunch of different names. Truth is, they're all built in the same factory, on the same assembly line."

"Oh—I'd wondered about that." Frank was paying close attention; after all, this was what he'd been urging me to do. "New ones cost about this much in the catalogs." I guess that's pretty close to a commitment, isn't it, when you start discussing money? It sounded like it to everyone else, too.

"We need room to deal. Don't worry, you'll get a good price."

"Count on it," promised Mom. She lived to negotiate.

Chapter 17

"I don't think I could ever deal like that," Tiffany said.

"You know it's true," I told my mom. "Most of us don't possess your killer instinct."

She sipped her diet cola and considered that. "We all have our talents, I suppose. The three of you certainly do."

"I'm not talented," declared Tiffany.

I couldn't let her get away with that. "Your brother says you write. Poetry and stuff."

She looked ready to kill me. Or Marlon. Or both.

Frank, who'd been working on his second chili dog, swallowed and asked, "Have you ever written, like, a song?"

She shook her head.

"I tried to," he continued. "Martin said it wasn't very good." He gave me a sidelong look.

I laughed. "I'm sure I'd do just as bad."

"Worse," said Frank.

"So why don't you try?" asked Mom. She was forever trying to get people to *do* things. I think too many things get done already.

"I'd like to hear," announced Tiffany getting back at me.

"I'll show you mine if you'll show me yours," I responded.

"It's time for some serious shopping," Mom decided. "Let's meet back here at, mmm," she looked at her watch, "four. Okay?"

"Not if we want to see a movie," Frank reminded her.

"Oh, yes. Make it three and then we'll decide."

"Doesn't your mother need to be back at the motel?" Tiffany asked me.

"Nothing to do on a Friday evening but check a few people in. My dad can handle that." Did she want to leave? "You told your folks we might be late, right?"

"Sure."

"No problem, then. Even if you watch that long English film," I nodded toward the poster, "We can still get going pretty early." Actually, I kind of wanted to see it.

"Yuck," said Frank.

"Double-yuck," agreed Tiffany. Apparently, neither was a romantic.

"We have a couple of hours. You hanging with us, Tiff?" I asked.

"I'm going to catch up with your mother," she replied.

That left Frank and me. "Tiffany's changed," he confided, as she walked away.

"Haven't we all?"

"Yeah, I guess." He looked thoughtful. Frank could do that, if he tried. "She used to be, oh, I don't know, kind of boring. It's like she was hiding who she was."

"And who she is has turned out to be a somewhat strange and scary person," I joked.

"A little," he agreed. "Almost as strange as you."

"You're not the most normal guy I ever met."

"Hey, 'The Strangers' would be a good name for a band."

"Been used, I'm pretty sure."

"All the good ones have," he complained. "You have any money left?"

"Some. I don't want to spend much. How 'bout you?"

"The same." He sounded unsure; it's hard to go to a mall and not blow a little cash. "I oughta look for some clothes."

"Wait for Christmas, man. You're on three more lists, now."

"Yeah!" He brightened. "Oh, but I gotta add three to *my* list."

"Nothing special," I warned, "For any of us. If you want to spend your money, spend it on your family."

"Okay," said Frank. "Let's go browse in 'Victoria's Secret' and bug the sales people."

"Who knows," I cracked, "We might find something for Tiffany." That kept us snickering for quite a while.

The idea may have appealed to us a bit, too. After all, we were teenage boys.

~

We didn't really spend any time, or money, on lingerie; we

didn't have the nerve. Frank and I window shopped our way around the mall, ending up in a book store.

I picked up a couple of books for myself and another for Dad; his birthday was coming up and he didn't wear ties anymore. Frank found himself a guitar mag. It wasn't one I care for—too full of heavy-metal guitar heroes. But Frank didn't think much of my favorite magazine, either, except for the equipment reviews. We both salivated over expensive axes.

Three o'clock found us back at the food court. Mom and Tiff were waiting at a table, surrounded by packages.

"Will you boys stow these in the wagon?" my mother asked. "And be sure to relock it."

"Sure, Mom. Meet you at the 'plex?" She nodded. "Grab some stuff, Frank."

"Don't we need the keys?"

"Mom has me carry a spare set, in case she loses hers," I answered.

"That was Martin's idea," explained Mom, "but we both worry about that kind of thing."

We hauled our loads out to the SUV. "Don't peek," I told Frank. "She's probably started her Christmas shopping."

"My mom doesn't do anything until December. It's always the last minute for her."

I heaved my packages into the back. "That would drive Mom crazy. Give me yours." I shoved them in. "That's it?" I closed the door and checked it. "Locked. Okay, let's go."

"You're that way, too," said Frank. "How does your dad stand you two?"

"He'd be lost without us. Drifting aimlessly," I claimed, "and enjoying every moment of it."

~

Frank, to no one's surprise, wanted comedy. I knew better than to suggest the British film, so I opted for sci-fi, even though most movies in that genre are pretty bad. All too often, they forget that

81

SF needs to be logical. We could have each gone our own way but it's no fun watching a movie by yourself.

"Okay," I said to Tiffany, "*you* choose."

She went for the slasher flick. I don't really like those; they give me nightmares.

Mom decided to shop some more. "I'll meet you after the show. Same place." She checked her watch. "That would be around five-thirty. We can all have a snack before we leave." As an afterthought, she added, "So don't waste your money on theater food."

But Frank said, "You can't watch without popcorn," and Tiffany's appetite rivals her brother's, so I was the only one who listened to Mom.

I sat down on one side of Tiff; Frank sat on the other. "Hey," he spouted, "this is almost like, you know, a date."

"Except Tiffany's too much woman for just one guy," I observed. "It gives a whole new meaning to double-dating."

That kept us from taking Frank's quip seriously. Tiff allowed me a touch of a smile, partly grateful, I think, partly embarrassed. Hard to tell; it was dark in there.

Tiffany doesn't let her emotions show that much, anyway. Not even one scream during the movie, while Frank was practically jumping up and down. I wondered whether she cried at sad films. I'll admit that I do.

And then the movie was over and soon the day was over and we were riding home through the dark. Heading back to the middle of nowhere.

Chapter 18

It was late, but we had to at least look at our purchases. I opened up the case on the restaurant floor and just admired my bass for a while.

"Now, what are you going to do with that?" asked Dad.

"We'll start a band," Frank answered for me.

"I don't know about that," I told him. "I might be a truly atrocious bass player."

I fumbled through a few notes. It really wasn't that different from the guitar.

Frank moved closer so he could hear. "That sounds pretty good, even without an amp."

"Must be the hollow body," I guessed. "Still needs to be plugged in."

"But not tonight," said Mom. "You can try out your amplifiers tomorrow."

"Okay." I didn't mind but Frank wanted to crank up, I'm sure. I slipped the bass back into its case.

"Have you named it yet?" Frank grinned at me. He thought of his guitar as a person and had named it "Twyla." He liked the name; he'd seen it in a magazine. He also knew that I considered it a really dopey idea.

"Mmm." I glanced over at my mom and it came to me. "Paula. Her name is Paula."

"I'm surprised you didn't call it Tiffany," Frank snickered.

I was immediately defensive and not certain why. "Any reason I'd do that?"

"You sure seem to like her a lot." Then he jabbed it in. "Must be true love."

I couldn't come up with anything.

"Oh, let the poor kid be," laughed my mom. "You did pay a lot of attention to Tiffany today," she said to me.

"He gave her the whole Martin show."

Mom smiled at Frank's crack. "For Martin, he was practically outgoing." She turned to me. "You hardly ever talk that much."

"I do with Frank." I looked at him. "And I'm definitely not in love with you."

That had everyone laughing. We all have our own methods of self-defense.

Later, falling asleep, I wondered: did I try to impress Tiffany? And I answered myself, honestly: sure. But why was a much more complicated question.

~

The deal Mom had worked out at the music store included two "combo" amps, both used, both basic and inexpensive. Mine was larger than Frank's; you need more power for a bass. I'd had more money to spend also. My savings covered bass and amp with no assistance from my parents.

Mom had said, "We promised to help with a classical guitar, nothing else." Cruel, but true: Mom's always the business woman. Still, I knew those matching funds might show up yet, sometime, somewhere.

Traffic had increased at the Hilltop Lodge. It was late October now, and trout were beginning to show up. So were trout fishermen. Most Saturday mornings, Frank was kept busy, between helping Dad at the dock and bussing in the restaurant. I worked in the restaurant, too, but had moved to the kitchen. Somewhere along the line, I'd taken over much of the cooking.

By early afternoon, things would slow down. The restaurant was closed and cleaned by then (and Amy had gone home). I usually had the rooms ready; if I needed help, Frank could assist me. Mom would start running laundry. The motel produced a lot of dirty linens, but mostly just towels and washcloths on Saturdays.

For lack of a better space, Frank and I had set our amps up in the bedroom. We were cramped and I didn't totally trust the wiring. It was as ancient as the building and ran through an old-fashioned fuse box. I'd never even seen a fuse before we moved there. As soon as we finished our work, we went up to try them out.

We had no instruction manual for Frank's amp. "I can figure it out," he said. "It's a lot like my little one."

"I have no idea what some of my controls do," I reported.

Frank took a look. "What's a 'compressor?'" he asked.

Fortunately, mine came with its original papers, though a bit tattered and grimy. We got them both working and produced some noise.

"I like it," Frank stated, "except for this 'tweed' covering."

"Prefer black?"

"Yeah, but for the price, I can live with it." I thought the tweed was pretty sharp, myself.

Once I got used to having four strings, instead of six, it was actually easy. My fingertips did get sore using steel strings; the calluses I'd developed on nylon weren't sufficient.

That evening, I e-mailed Rita to tell her all that I'd been up to. It had been a while and I didn't want to lose touch. She was the only connection left to where and what I'd been before Ruby. I promised her I'd keep up on the guitar. I guess I felt some guilt about letting so many other things take priority.

I'd let a little self-pity slip in, too. At times, I still missed my life in Atlanta. It had been simpler.

~

Amy had shown little interest, Saturday morning, in hearing about our trip. She chattered on about a variety of subjects, especially her day in the woods. But Amy's always talking and we were busy so most of it, I'm afraid, didn't make an impression.

By Sunday, she'd had a chance to spend some time with Tiffany. It had given her ideas.

"Are you and Frank really going to have a band?"

I had sort of gone along with Frank's plan, without actually committing. "I guess so. If two people makes a band."

"Maybe you could back me up. It would be a lot better than singing along to a tape."

"Well, we might use a singer," I replied, coming at it from a different angle. The nuance was not lost on Amy.

"Don't get conceited before you've even learned how to play," she laughed. Then, out of the blue, came, "Tiffany should be in it."

"In the band?" I turned over the eggs I was frying and turned to face her. "Doing what?"

"She's always banging on Marlon's drums when she gets the chance. Don't burn those." She nodded toward the griddle.

"Okay. Grits—" I plopped a mound on each plate. "Eggs. Sausage gravy—and the toast. Here you go." I handed them to her and she went up front.

Did Amy really believe that Tiffany could, or even wanted to, play? Or was she just trying to involve her friend?

The next time Amy came into the kitchen, I asked "Do you think Tiff could be talked into playing? I don't want to embarrass her by asking outright." I didn't want to embarrass myself, either.

"I'll work on it," she promised.

~

"I've written another song," announced Frank.

I'd spent all Sunday afternoon cleaning motel rooms while he sat watching over the dock, guitar in hands.

"Let's hear it," I said. "Is it better than the last one?"

"Lots."

Well, it was better than the last one, which consisted of two chords and yelling. This one was three chords and yelling.

"Not bad." I was too tired to fake enthusiasm. "Hey, do you think we need a drummer?"

"Sure. Sooner or later." He looked around. "But we couldn't fit one in this room."

"We could throw out some of your junk."

Frank paid no attention; he was busy digging for a catalog. "Look here," he said, holding it open. "Electronic drums. You can carry the whole thing under your arm. Or," he leafed over a few pages, "a drum machine. Then you don't need a drummer at all."

"Gol-ly! What'll they come up with next?"

"Drum machines aren't new," Frank answered, quite seriously.

"You're a tough audience," I sighed. I looked up at the clock. "Time for dinner."

We clattered down the stairs in the cool evening air. The apartment was reached only by an outside staircase, roofed over but still pretty much open to the elements.

"What was all that noise upstairs?" asked Dad. "You sounded like a really bad punk-rock band."

"The kind you used to take me to see, dear," Mom reminded him.

"Ah, we were young and still had our hearing."

"And you had a thing for Patti Smith."

Frank had no idea who that was. Not because it was too far back. He liked bands like "Boston" but was hazy on other music from that era.

"Is that what you were trying for?" Dad almost sounded hopeful; trying to regain his youth or some similar cliché.

I looked at Frank and Frank looked at me. Neither of us had thought seriously about that kind of thing. We were just goofing around.

I shrugged. "The only thing we've ever practiced is surf music."

"But that's not what we want to play. Right?" Frank didn't sound completely sure of me.

"No." I shook my head. "Though we can do 'Walk, Don't Run' properly now."

"That would make a good show-piece," Mom pointed out, "Regardless of what else you play." She was thinking *way* ahead of us.

"Yeah," agreed Frank, "if we had a drummer."

"I'm working on it," I assured him.

Chapter 19

"You're a friend of J.R. Akin, aren't you?"

"Guess so. I know him." Billie Peale had never come up to me and started a conversation before, even though we sat side-by-side, playing flute, in the band.

"Yeah. I heard you worked out with him." She looked doubtful.

"Just once in a while. Really shows, doesn't it?" I quipped. Our abilities were too far apart to actually work out together.

That got her to lighten up, a bit. She sat down and started fingering her instrument. "Is he strong?"

I shrugged. "Compared to me, yes."

"How 'bout Shawn Curtiss?"

"Oh. I think J.R. could probably lift more weight. Better leverages."

She gave me a questioning look.

"He's shorter, bigger boned, deeper chested." Mr. Edwards had explained all this to me. "Shawn's got those long arms and legs so his muscles have to work harder to lift the same weight." I was curious. "What's up, anyway?"

"Nothing, really. They're sort of rivals, you know, and people argue about who's the better athlete." She leafed through her music. "Most of my friends say Shawn." Because they were black; she knew I understood that.

Though the racial thing existed at Pinelands, it usually wasn't a big deal. Blacks and whites were more likely to date than to fight.

Still, race (or ethnicity or culture or whatever word you want to use) was a factor in who hung with whom. And everyone wants to belong somewhere. Even the most ardent loner, deny it as he will, has the urge.

The bell rang and Mr. Montero called class to order.

~

"There's a deputy pulling up out front," I observed. "What

have you done now?" Frank and I were doing homework in the restaurant—more room to spread out.

"Which one?" he asked, not looking up from his math problems.

"Hasn't got out yet. Ah, it's your buddy, Buddy."

Deputy Ortiz came in. "Hello, boys. Are Mr. and Mrs. Groves around?"

"No, sir, they went to a meeting." Ruby River Small Business Association or something like that.

"We're in charge," chimed in Frank.

"That's okay. I just stopped to see how you were doing," he told Frank. "Happy here?" The deputy pulled out a chair and sat in it backwards, like the guys in old Westerns.

"Sure," said Frank. He grinned at me. "Even though they make me work a lot."

"We only wanted you as slave labor," I informed him.

"Yeah, but you don't have to chain me to the bed at night!"

"Be thankful you *have* a bed."

Ortiz looked from one of us to the other; I think he was amused. "It sounds like you get along pretty well."

Yeah, we did. We'd gotten close.

"Do you intend to stay?"

Frank nodded his head. "Everyone's better off this way. My mom and Bill get along great, now." According to Jason, but he liked Bill. Liked having his own room, too. "I guess they mostly fought about me."

It's hard to follow up a statement like that. "Hmm. Bill Watson has a, uh, temper, doesn't he?" asked Deputy Ortiz.

Frank laughed. "He gets mad and punches holes in the wall. Mom had to take him to the emergency room once for a broken hand." He got serious. "But he's never hit anyone." Then, taking us totally by surprise: "Do you like my mother?"

"Um, why, I—" The deputy regained some composure. "Why do you ask that?"

"Martin thinks you're in love with her." He smirked at me.

"Urk," I said. I don't know whether Deputy Ortiz or I was more disconcerted.

"Well," he started, "your mother and I go way back but we were never friends or anything. I was just the fat Mexican kid and she was—she moved in a different circle." The deputy got up. "You look a lot like her," he said, "but tall, like your father."

"Were you a friend of my dad?" Frank sounded hopeful.

"Ah, not exactly." The deputy sounded embarrassed. "Fact is, we pretty much hated each other. Your mother holds that against me, I'm sure," he continued, "especially since I beat him up a couple times." He looked downright ashamed of himself. I don't think Deputy Ortiz liked to lose control of his emotions. His role model was probably Joe Friday. "That was back in high school. I never saw him again after I joined the army."

He took half a step toward Frank. "I figured you should know the story on that. Okay?"

Frank nodded. "Sure."

Deputy Ortiz turned. "I'll be on my way. Take care, guys." He paused. "And take care of each other." I know that's a cliché but he sounded like he meant it.

~

"You and Shawn Curtiss have some kind of rivalry going?" I questioned J.R., as soon as he finished his set.

"Aw, that's gotten way blown up," he replied, when he got his breath back. "We just push each other."

"Curtiss? I've had him in a few classes." Edwards came in as a substitute teacher on a fairly regular basis. "Tall kid. On the football team with you, isn't he?"

"Yeah. You gonna do your set?" J.R. was normally very polite around adults but that disappeared when he worked out.

I still dropped by occasionally, more to talk art with Mr. Edwards than to lift weights. He had suggested that I would probably do better with brief, infrequent workouts, anyway, since I don't gain weight easily. I'd just burn out if I tried to emulate J.R.

Frank wouldn't accompany me. He'd tried it once and decided it was boring.

"We'll be on the team again next year," said J.R., as his partner finished lifting. "And both go out for baseball this spring but I'm leaving basketball to Shawn." He sat down on the bench. "I could play but I'd rather use this season to add muscle." He pumped out some dumbbell presses.

"You're stronger than Shawn," I stated.

"But he can run faster. Jump a tad higher, too."

"Maybe, years from now, your picture will be in the trophy case along side Buddy Ortiz."

"The deputy?" asked Mr. Edwards.

"Same guy," answered J.R. "My father knows him pretty well. He could have played college ball but passed it up to join the military."

That was a new piece of info. "Seems to have worked out okay for him."

"If you want to stay around here for the rest of your life. I intend to get a scholarship *and* use it." J.R. sounded emphatic.

~

Amy slipped into her bus seat and motioned for me to come back.

"A pretty girl beckons," I told my friends. "I must away."

Robby sort of snorted.

I sat down in the seat in front of her. "What's going on?" I asked.

"Can you come by my place later?"

"Should be able to. By myself?"

"If possible." She was sensitive to Frank's situation. "But it's okay if you can't ditch Frank."

"All right. I'll call if I can't make it. Is this about anything special?"

"I'll tell you then." She wouldn't say more: an unusual occurrence with Amy. But this invitation was more than unusual. It had never happened before.

I went back to my seat. Frank didn't say anything but I could see he was curious.

"Hey, man, Amy wants me at some kind of secret meeting when we get home," I told him. "Mind if I leave you behind?"

"As long as you tell me everything later."

"Every lurid detail." Then I whispered "I think it has to do with Tiff." She was seated by Amy now and I didn't want her to overhear.

"You've never been to her home, have you?" asked Robby.

"No. It's the trailer by her bus stop?"

"That's it," said Frank. "The white one with the green trim."

"And the extra room tacked on the side," added Rob.

"They've never been able to stop the roof from leaking where they attached it." Frank smiled at the thought. "Every time it rains hard, the buckets come out."

"Gee, the weather's clear today," I remarked. "I'm gonna miss that."

Chapter 20

"That was quick," said Amy. "You must have really hurried."

"I have a fast bike." And I'd taken off almost as soon as I got home.

"Leave it here. We're walking over to Tiffany's; I want time to talk." I never even got to see the inside of Amy's home. She'd been sitting on the front porch when I arrived.

"Does she know we're coming?"

"She knows *I'm* coming."

The Theos lived only a few blocks away. That was Ruby for you: trashy trailers next to mini-mansions. I leaned my bike against her porch.

There were no sidewalks here so we walked on the roadway, to avoid sandspurs. They seemed to grow everywhere. It was one block down, two blocks over (that would put us by the river), then down one more block.

"I hear that Tiff's not the only one who writes poems," Amy told me.

"Yeah," I said, sounding more sheepish than I wanted, "but even Frank's written poetry, if you count his songs."

"Really?" she laughed. "I hope I never hear any of it."

"That's mean," I replied, but I was laughing too.

She shifted to another subject. "Is he a good guitar player?"

"Hmm. In a—limited way, yeah."

"Nothing like you, though, huh?" I knew she was mocking me a bit. The way I talk sometimes, I probably deserved it.

"Oh, I'm limited, too," I maintained.

"You're good." She was serious now. "I've heard you."

"All I really know is classical—one limited style. Actually," I continued, "I'm not much ahead of Frank when it comes to anything else."

She stopped and looked at me. "You run yourself down too much." A little smile appeared on her heart-shaped face. "Just like Tiffany."

~

The Theos lived in a "stilt house." That is, all the living quarters were upstairs and the bottom floor was not enclosed. A lot of the houses near the river were built like that, because of the possibility of flooding.

"Tiff's mom will be shocked," giggled Amy. "Boys *never* visit her."

"Oh? Do they all go to your house, instead?" It was meant as a joke, mostly, and she took it that way.

"My mom has to beat 'em away from the door with a broom," she answered "and if that doesn't work, Dad has a shotgun!"

We went up the front stairs. It was a big place, done in unpainted cedar.

Tiffany's mother answered the door. "Hello, Amy," she said. "Why, hello, Martin. This is a surprise." Mrs. Theo remembered everybody's name, even if they'd met only once. She looked at me, uncertainly. "Was Tiffany expecting you?"

Amy shook her head and smiled. "No," she whispered, like she was letting Mrs. Theo in on a conspiracy. Amy tended toward the dramatic.

I sort of shrugged. "Amy's idea, Mrs. Theo," I explained. "Is Marlon home?"

"Not yet," she replied. "Tiffany's in her room, I believe." She hesitated and then decided it was okay. "Amy knows the way," she told me. "The two of them spend a lot of time in there."

"It's much larger than mine," said Amy, "but her decor's gotten depressing."

"Don't I know it," sighed Mrs. Theo. "At least she hasn't taken to wearing black."

Amy took a left and led me down a hall. "That's Marlon's room," she said of the first door we passed. It looked large, but normal.

"You'd better let her know I'm with you," I said in a low voice, "before we go barging in."

"Good idea. She keeps her door locked, anyway."

She knocked at the next door. "Hey, Tiff, it's Amy." She glanced over at me. "And I brought someone."

~

"I see what you mean about the decor," I commented to Amy. I didn't try to keep Tiff from hearing; I thought it might get her started talking. Besides, she knew by now not to take me seriously.

I was right. Tiffany gestured toward Amy. "Her bedroom is all pink pillows and lace and flowers." She looked approvingly around her own room. "I was never much on that stuff."

"That's true," agreed Amy, "But I don't get this, at all."

Tiff's tastes had apparently taken a turn toward the Gothic. Not the full black candles trip but a tad grim, none the less.

"It's just a phase," I told Amy, facetiously. "She'll grow out of it." Surprisingly, Tiffany laughed.

"You're probably right," she said. "I'm already getting bored with this look."

Tiffany had been very cool when she saw me at the door, like she'd been expecting me all along. It simply wasn't her style to act surprised. Tiff was going to relock the door (she really valued her privacy) but Amy and I felt Mrs. Theo would be happier if we left it ajar. In all honesty, I'd be more comfortable, too. I think Tiffany would just as soon have bugged her mom.

I sat down at her desk while Amy perched on the end of the bed. "No computer?" I asked Tiffany.

"I can use the one in Daddy's office," she replied.

"That's at the end of the hall," added Amy. Marlon has one, also. I come over to use them." She looked at her friend and shook her head. "Tiff prefers to write longhand."

"It is more personal," I noted, "and more private."

"I'd waste far too much time if I had a computer in here," stated Tiffany, "or a TV."

"But music's okay, huh?"

She had an impressive stereo and plenty of CDs. All neatly shelved, too; I liked that.

"Play something, Tiff," Amy requested. "Something that's not too depressing." Tiffany picked some jangly folk-pop.

"It's not country but I know you like it," she said to Amy. "This okay with you, Marlon?"

Amy giggled.

"Martin," I said.

"Hmm? Oh, did I—I did, didn't I?" Tiffany gave me an embarrassed smile. "You remind me of him, sometimes."

"And the names sound similar," Amy pointed out.

"Yeah, I guess so. Makes a good segue, anyway." I wanted to change the subject. "Have you given Marlon anything to print yet?"

That brought a definite reaction. She hadn't made up her mind, I think, and didn't like being pushed. "No," she shot back, "have you?" I was just as reluctant, I admitted.

"Read him something, Tiff," urged Amy.

Now came Tiffany's chance to counter-attack. "You promised to show me yours," she reminded me, "if I let you see mine."

"I hope your mother's not listening to this," I cracked. "She'll never let me in the house again."

That broke Amy up. Soon, we were all laughing.

"One poem," decided Tiffany, sobering a bit, "and you have to promise to bring something of yours." I did.

She leafed through a folder and chose a piece, written on notebook paper. Then, impulsively, she thrust it toward me.

"You read it."

"Coward," Amy accused her, between giggles.

The poem was dark and full of melodramatic imagery. It was the Tiffany inside on display. No wonder she was uncertain about sharing it.

I looked up at Tiff. "I can't do free verse. My stuff always develops a structure, despite all my intentions."

"Do they rhyme?" asked Amy. "Tiff's poems never do."

"Not usually. Blank verse," I explained. She looked puzzled.

"Amy's blank, too," smiled Tiffany. "I don't think she knows the difference."

Amy was miffed. "Don't act so superior. You don't do it to anyone else."

"I've seen her treat Frank like that; she must like him." Amy laughed at that. "Anyway," I told her, "I mean they have a regular pattern to them, like a song. You could never sing this." I handed the sheet back to Tiffany.

"Well, did you like it?" demanded Amy.

Tiff looked like she didn't approve of the question but wanted to hear the answer.

"Uh, yeah, I think so." That was probably the best thing I could say; it sounded honest and it was. "But it's very personal." I looked at Tiff. "I don't do that much, either."

"Then what's the point?" she asked.

~

Though I pretty much knew what the point was, I didn't want to debate Tiffany on it. But, on my way home, I thought it through.

It's no good just to go on about what's inside of you. There's a whole world going on outside of you too. The interesting stuff happens when inside meets outside.

Chapter 21

"I may have us a drummer."

Frank gave me a suspicious look. "You don't mean Marlon, do you?"

"Nope. Right family, though."

"Tiffany? She can't play."

"Neither can we," I reminded him. "Not very well."

"What's she gonna play? Will she buy a drum set?" Frank was thinking this through.

"Hey, she hasn't even agreed for sure. She just said she might come and jam with us." Tiff had been pretty noncommittal; so would I, in the same situation. "She sounded okay on Marlon's snare."

"Can she borrow it?"

"Don't know."

"We'll see," said Frank. "I wouldn't mind having Tiff in the 'Frank Hanley Trio.'"

"You mean the 'Martin Groves Combo,'" I responded.

~

"Is your brother coming for Thanksgiving?" asked Frank.

"No, not enough time." I was at the computer, composing a letter. "We will have to fit him in here at Christmas."

"No way. Tell him to sleep in the tree house."

"Okay, let me add that. 'Frank says you'll have to spend Christmas break in the tree house. Don't worry, it doesn't freeze most nights.'" I turned my chair around. "That sound good?"

"Yeah, fine," he said. His mind was already somewhere else. "How long will he stay? A couple weeks?"

"More, I think. They take longer breaks at college."

"I could move out," he offered, "for a while."

"No, you can't, man. We'll fit Jeff in. Lots of room for a roll-away in here." I rotated back to face the screen. "But we'll make him bring it up the stairs." I typed a few words. "Did you want to be with your family? I mean, for Christmas?"

"I don't know. Maybe."

"It's not like they're far away. You can spend Christmas at both places." I looked over my message. "I guess this is ready to send. Do you want to e-mail anyone, while I'm on line?"

"Like who?"

"We could send to Tiff," I suggested, "except I don't know her address. Remind me to ask."

"Uh-huh. Robby has a computer."

"He's not hooked up. His parents are afraid of the Internet."

"Face it, we're a couple of losers, with no friends," joked Frank, "stuck in the middle of nowhere." He'd picked up my line.

"We might find you a girlfriend on the net," I said, "but not tonight. I have something else to do." I closed the browser and popped in a CD.

"Do you think my mom would want me at home for Christmas?" He was still thinking about that.

"Sure, but what if you start fighting again?"

"Yeah." Frank sounded resigned. "That would ruin it."

"People get edgy around the holidays, you know. I might take a swing at you, myself," I admitted, "if Jeff doesn't first!"

"It would take both of you." Frank had been sitting, cross legged, on the bed. Now he got up. "What's that?" he asked, looking at the screen.

"Poems. I need to choose one." I'd told him of my promise to Tiffany.

Frank pulled up a chair beside me. "That one's really dorky."

"Gee, thanks." He was right, of course.

"Girls go for sappy stuff like that," he said, like he was an authority or something.

"Tiff doesn't. She'd think it was dorky, too. She just wouldn't say so." I thought a moment. "Well, maybe she would."

I scrolled to the next page. "This would be safer."

Frank squinted at it. "Supposed to be funny?"

"'Witty' is the word," I replied.

"Yeah," he said, "it sounds like the way you talk, sort of." He looked like he had an idea. "It's almost a country song." He pointed to the screen. "This first part could be, like, the chorus."

"Uh-huh." I could see it. "I'll print this one."

"Print me a copy, too."

~

Amy had *The Grizzly*, the school newspaper. She grabbed her usual seat, two rows back from me, opposite side.

"Did you see this?" she asked, holding it open.

I shook my head. I hadn't picked one up, yet, but Frank had a copy and I grabbed it. "What page?" I called to Amy.

"Six," she replied, "at the bottom."

I leafed to it. "There," Frank said, pointing.

It was the announcement of a school talent show. "That's a while, yet," said Frank. The date was mid-January.

"A lot goes on the next couple of months," I replied. "May get here sooner than you think."

Robby sat down. He looked ready to burst.

"Did you hear about the fight?"

I nodded. The story had been spreading.

"What fight?" Frank asked.

"Paul Clemmons and some black kid. Will—I forget his last name."

"Fat guy? Will Dudley?" suggested Frank.

"Yeah, that's him."

"They're both kind of hefty," I remarked. "They don't look much like fighters."

"It didn't look much like a fight, I hear," said Rob, "but they'll both get suspended."

Tiffany had arrived. She was always one of the last to board but Amy would save her a seat. They talked to each other for a while, voices low, as we started home. Then Tiffany pulled out my poem and passed it to Amy. I'd given her the copy in band class.

I hadn't told her she could show it to Amy but I hadn't told her not to, either. I'd known they shared everything. Anyway, I wasn't going to say anything and attract attention on the bus.

Amy laughed and held it up. "I like this, Martin." Oh, great.

Tiff smiled just a bit, a little twist at the corner of her mouth. She knew I was embarrassed but she wouldn't rub it in.

"Can I give this to Marlon?" she asked, softly, taking the paper from her friend.

"Only if he gets one of yours, too." I responded.

"Okay," said Tiffany.

~

"Do you think Amy's pretty?"

A loaded question, to be sure. Mrs. Akin had come to the Lodge to clean fish and brought Amy and Tiffany with her. Now, Tiff sat on the dock with Frank and me, while Amy helped her mom.

"Um, she's—cute."

"Yeah, cute," agreed Frank.

"Good cheekbones," I offered. "Maybe when she loses a little 'baby fat.'"

Frank snickered at that.

"Hey, don't be mean." I elbowed him. "She's only a tad on the plump side. People do grow out of that."

"My nose is too big," Tiffany blurted.

"It's a nice nose," I stated. "I couldn't imagine you without it."

"Your glasses would slide right off your face," said Frank. Then, a little more thoughtfully, "No, I really like your nose. You look like Cher."

I gave her the once-over. "Yeah, except for your hair." Which was wavy and brown. "And the glasses. Why don't you wear contacts, like Marlon?"

"You don't like my glasses?" It wasn't a serious question; she was just shifting the subject.

"They're beautiful glasses. Aren't they, Frank?"

"I like the ones that turn up at the corners. With rhinestones." Tiffany wore wire rims.

"Why am I here with you idiots?"

"To protect Amy?" suggested Frank.

"Or, maybe, to protect us *from* Amy," I said.

"Like either of you needs to worry," sniffed Tiffany. "Amy's a boy magnet. She already has more guys hanging around than she knows what to do with."

That was something of an exaggeration, though Amy was certainly popular.

"Do you get the extras?" Frank asked, with an innocent expression

"No. They're even worse idiots than you two."

~

Will Dudley and Paul Clemmons were pretty much bottom men in their respective cliques. Unpopular, unathletic kids who shot their mouths off too much, trying to impress someone— maybe themselves. I felt uncomfortable around guys like that because I recognized a little of them in me.

The difference was that I'd been able to step back and take a look at things. I'd rather not try to fit in that way. Better a loner than a loser.

It seems they'd been bad-mouthing each other and, with a little encouragement from their "friends," had gotten into it during lunch period. The result was a two week, "in-school" suspension; they'd be sitting in the same room all day for a while. Neither had suffered any damage.

To most, the fight was a joke. Still, there was friction, no doubt about it, between some of the blacks and some of the cowboys.

Chapter 22

Sometimes, it's easier to communicate by modem than face-to-face. Once I got Tiffany's address, we e-mailed each other regularly.

I mentioned this to Mom and she went a different way with it. "I think we should have a web site, once your father starts guiding. For the motel, too."

"You'd share it?"

"Yes. There's not much to say about the Lodge, anyway. All the news concerns fishing."

Frank, who'd been busy with some frozen yogurt, broke in.

"We should have a site for, you know, the band."

"You gonna pay for it?" I asked.

"There are lots of places we could have a free page."

My mom looked thoughtful. "Free is good. But a professional site might be a good investment," she said, "if you ever get this so-called band going."

"Don't be skeptical," I told her. "It takes time."

"We're playing in the talent show," Frank promised, "one way or another."

"You haven't picked a name, yet," Mom reminded us.

"He won't decide until Tiffany agrees to play," said Frank, "but I've been making a list."

"Me, too," I admitted. "Hey, let's go look for band web sites. We might get some ideas."

"Yeah. Think 'The Malfunction' will have a site?"

They did. It was pretty simple: pictures of the members, some reviews.

"That's boring," complained Frank. "Try that link."

It led to a site covering the area music scene.

"There are a lot of bands," I remarked.

Frank had an answer for that. "College town. Hey, a bulletin board." There were lots of musicians seeking bands and bands seeking musicians.

"Everyone seems to need drummers," Frank noted. He hesitated, then said, "I know a guy at school that drums. He might want to play with us."

"Can he get here for practice? We couldn't go to Blessed."

"Don't know. It was just an idea."

~

We'd seen a lot less of Robby since hunting season started. Almost every weekend, he was out in the woods. And almost every Monday morning, he had to tell us about it. It really drove in how far apart our interests were.

I have nothing against hunters, you understand. I can even see the "becoming part of nature" thing some of them will go on about. I'm just not into it, myself.

Robby showed about as much interest in our music. He was disappointed, too, when we continued to turn down his invitations. I thought Frank might have gone for the idea but, between work and all the other stuff we were trying to do, neither of us seemed to have the time.

"We can get by without you, one weekend," I told him. "I can cover." It wasn't me Rob wanted along, anyway.

Frank shook his head. He would have liked to spend some time with his buddy, I'm sure, but something was preventing him. He sat and let it build up for a while.

Then it came out. "I'm not going to stay in the woods with Robby's parents. They think I'm—they don't like me. It's nasty out there, too, and—and I don't like killing things." He seemed relieved to have admitted it.

I didn't know whether to let Robby in on this. It was a confidence. Maybe now, having told me, Frank would find it easier to say something to his friend.

~

"It looks like Jekyll and Hyde live here," was Tiffany's opinion, on seeing our bedroom. "I can guess who's Jekyll and who's Hyde."

"Is she insulting me?" asked Frank.

"Not necessarily. Maybe she likes slobs."

Tiff had arranged to have the bus drop her at the Lodge this afternoon. All day, she'd been carrying around a large zippered bag; it was too big to stow in her locker.

She opened it now. "This is just a toy," she said, pulling out a small keyboard. "It was Marlon's but it's been gathering dust.

"Here, plug this in." Tiffany handed me a "wall-wart" AC adapter. "It includes a drum machine of sorts." She turned on one of the built-in rhythms.

"Gee, that's cheesy sounding," I remarked.

"Might be better through some real speakers," Frank suggested. "Those are tiny."

"I can also play drums on the keys." Tiff laid out a simple kick-snare pattern. "But it's clumsy."

I agreed. "That would never work for a live performance."

Frank had been checking out the instrument. "Let's hear some of the voices."

Now, Tiff got shy. "I don't know how to play," she objected.

"That never stopped either of us," I assured her. "Anyway, we just want to see how they sound."

She ran through the voices. Some weren't bad, some truly stank.

"Too bad you can't play," said Frank. "The organ sounds cool." Especially, hooked up to my amp.

"So do the strings," I added, "but they're easy." I reached over Tiff's shoulder. "You can just hold high notes, like this." I played an octave, then a fifth.

Tiffany turned to look at me. "That actually sounds good."

"I didn't know you could play keyboard," commented Frank.

"I can't. I read how to do that in a magazine."

Tiffany reached into her bag. "All I need are these to practice." She pulled out a pair of drumsticks. "And a cardboard box or something. I brought this, too." Out came a tambourine.

"Any more goodies?" I asked.

"No. I have claves and maracas and some other rhythm stuff. I thought this was enough, for now."

"So we still need some real drums," Frank observed.

"Why don't you show her a catalog?"

"Sure." He dug a couple out. "But let's not forget to try playing together."

We plugged in and fooled around for a while. Tiff could keep time, which was all that really mattered.

Then, we attempted a song that Frank liked; it was laid out in "tab" in one of his guitar magazines.

"Who's gonna sing?" he asked, innocently.

Although Frank didn't have much of a voice, he enjoyed singing. Mine was okay but ordinary. I could go a lot higher than Frank.

We both looked at Tiffany.

She practically panicked. "Not me," she protested. "No way."

"She's shy," said Frank, "like you." He turned to Tiff. "I can't get him to sing, either."

"It's hard to perform for just a few friends," I told him. "It's much easier to get up in front of an audience. You don't know them."

"Oh, Mr. Showbiz," he laughed.

"I had to give guitar recitals. I know."

"You never told me that. Was it a big audience?"

I shook my head. "Mostly families of the students."

We worked through the song, with Frank singing. There wasn't any melody to speak of, so it didn't matter.

"What we need to do is write a song together," Frank decided. "You're both good with words." He gave us a questioning look. "How come you're better at writing words than saying them?"

Tiff and I synchronized our shrugs.

"Maybe we like more time to think," she suggested.

"Could be," I agreed, "and we don't want to let the words out until they're just right."

"In other words, you're afraid of saying something stupid." Frank flashed one of his silly smiles. "That never bothered me."

~

"Tiff has a good voice," Marlon confided. "Not that you'll ever hear it. I only know from listening through the wall."

"Oh, what does she sing?" I tried to imagine. Folk songs? Rock ballads? Opera?

"Whatever's playing on her stereo. She sings along." He tapped his snare drum as he turned a tuning key. "It's usually hard to drag any information out of her but she was pretty talkative last night. She even had to show me those electronic drums." Frank had actually lent her one of his precious catalogs.

Mr. Montero left the band room open during lunch period. Students could come in to practice or just hang out until class started. I'd taken to doing that more often since the weather had turned cooler.

"Think she'll buy a set? Some of them are really cheap."

"She seemed more enthusiastic about the keyboard, now. Played it all evening. I think I even heard her sing along."

"We've created a monster," I joked. "But, seriously, she probably didn't read music well enough, before. I know she wasn't very good at it when she started band."

"Good point," said Marlon. "Now, you may need to look for another drummer."

"Are you volunteering?" Why not ask, I thought.

"Well, no," he answered. "You couldn't depend on me." I'd figured as much. "And I would inhibit Tiff."

"Oh, right, I suppose you would." That, I hadn't considered. "This is her chance to outshine you, isn't it?"

"Yeah," Marlon chuckled. "It's about time."

Chapter 23

"I talked with Bill Watson this morning," said Dad. "He seems okay to me."

We were in the laundry room, behind the kitchen, Mom and Dad and I. Dad had left Frank in charge of the dock, I guess so he could talk to us privately.

"What did he want?" Mom had formed a bad opinion of the man and it showed.

"To check on Frank," Dad responded, "and to see if he'd come to Thanksgiving dinner."

I immediately gave my thoughts. "He should go."

Mom nodded. "Yes, certainly."

"Bill's not an articulate guy. I can see why he'd have trouble dealing with a smart-mouth like Frank." He grinned at me. "Around here we just smart-mouth back at him."

"That's not an excuse," protested Mom, "but I think Julie's just as much to blame."

"Bill always takes her side," I said. "I mean, when she argues with Frank."

"Hmm. Afraid to overstep his authority?" mused Dad. Teacher-think.

"What authority? Ms. Differs gets her way pretty much all the time."

"That doesn't sound like a very healthy relationship. I wouldn't let your mother get away with it."

Mom laughed. "Not that you could stop me. Really, though, if he lets himself be controlled like that, it's no wonder he blows up sometimes. But that's not an excuse, either."

~

"This is Jimi," said Frank. I found out later it was spelled like Hendrix. "Jimi Peale."

"Hi. Peale?"

"Yeah. I'm Billie's brother," he told me. "She's mentioned you. Says you don't talk much."

"What?" I paused. "Me?"

Another pause. "I—talk—sometimes."

"That is really dumb," Frank commented.

Jimi cracked up. I could tell I was going to like this guy.

"Anyone who laughs at my jokes is fine with me," I said to Frank. "Talent is secondary."

Jimi had been waiting when we arrived at school; he was Frank's prospective drummer. They saw each other a lot during the day but I had only a few minutes before class started.

"You have a kit?" I asked. Apparently, they both regarded me as the "leader."

He nodded. "It's old and beat up but it sounds good."

"And you can play? I mean, the basic stuff?"

"Uh-huh. Can you?" he countered, with a smile.

"More or less. So, how do we get together to try it out?"

"Jimi could take the bus with us. If he doesn't have a ride home, he could stay overnight, couldn't he?" asked Frank.

"Sure, but what about the drums?"

"I could just bang on whatever's around."

"Like Tiffany did."

"Okay, you two set it up," I said. "But speaking of Tiff, she still owns the drummer spot if she wants it. Right?"

"Yeah, yeah," Frank agreed, "whatever."

~

It was only right to inform Tiffany and I did, at lunch. Amy might have suggested it only because she felt she was neglecting her friend but now I was committed to having Tiff in the band.

"No matter what you choose to play," I told her. "You don't have to be a drummer."

"I know. Maybe one drummer in the family is enough."

"But if you want it, it's yours. We don't know if this kid, Jimi, is any good," I pointed out, "or dependable."

"Ask his sister," she suggested. "She'll be honest."

"Okay. I'm going over to the band room. Coming?"

Tiffany accompanied me. She usually didn't.

Billie was already there, engrossed in homework. She was seated on the floor, top riser, leaning against the wall.

"Hey, Smarty," she greeted me, as Tiff and I approached. Yeah, the name had inevitably followed me. "How are you at geometry?"

"Straight As," I admitted. I'd loved geometry. I guess it was the logic involved. The same can't be said for algebra.

"What's wrong with this?"

She was trying to prove a theorem. I pointed out her mistake. It seemed obvious to me but I knew better than to say so.

Tiffany didn't speak a word. She just sat quietly in a chair and watched us.

"I met your brother this morning."

"Huh?" Billie looked up from her paper. "Oh, he said he was going to talk to you."

"Yeah, about playing drums with my friends and me." I gestured toward Tiff. "Tiffany, here, and Frank Hanley. Tell me," I asked, "how well does he play?"

"Fact is, he's really good."

"Uh-oh," said Tiff, with a smile. Billie gave her a quizzical glance.

"As a group, we're pretty incompetent," I told her.

"It won't matter. He just wants to play," Billie responded. "It's all he thinks about."

I sighed. "Another Frank," I said to Tiffany.

~

"When do you eat Thanksgiving dinner at your house?" I asked Frank.

"Oh, like, mid-afternoon."

"Perfect. We'll be waiting until after dark. You can have two dinners!"

"Yeah," he said. "How 'bout you coming to my place?"

"Maybe, if I'm not too busy. We're booked up the whole weekend, you know. Have you asked your Mom?"

"Not yet."

"I wouldn't want to show up if I wasn't expected."

Frank shrugged. "No one would notice. They're too busy with football."

Neither of us was a big sports fan. I occasionally watched some baseball and Frank was a pro wrestling junkie, but that doesn't count.

"Jimi wants to come tomorrow," said Frank. "Think that's okay?"

"Fine," I replied, "if it clears with my folks."

"They won't mind that he's black, will they?"

I laughed. "No way. They is sophisty-kated cosmopolitans. Is he going to ride home with us?" I looked around the bus. "That'll be a first."

"Uh-huh. His sister's going to pick him up. She drives."

"Some of these guys," said Robby, nodding toward the back of the bus, "might give him a hard time. Or you."

"They've always given me a hard time," Frank answered.

"Do you know Jimi?" I asked Rob.

"Yeah. I'm in some of his classes, same as Frank. He gets in trouble a lot."

"Nothing bad," explained Frank. "Just cuts up in class."

"He has—what do you call it, Frank?"

"Attention deficit?"

"Right. Once he broke into a drum solo on his desk top in the middle of a test. Remember that?"

Frank nodded. "But he's a good guy," he said to me. "You'll like him."

~

"Listen to this," Frank told me. It was an unusually warm afternoon and we were up in the tree house. Frank had brought his guitar and mini-amp. He started playing, and then singing, a song.

"Hey, that's one of my poems," I said.

"Yep." He went into the second verse.

I looked at the paper he was playing from. It was just lyrics and chord names, since Frank didn't read music. When he finished, I asked to borrow his instrument.

"The chorus may sound too much like the verses. Maybe if you did this—" I changed a chord. "And then back—"

"What was that? A-minor? Cool."

"But the lyrics suck," I responded.

"I know," said Frank. "Too artsy."

"I never intended for them to be a song. I never intended for you to go snooping in my files, either."

I wasn't mad and Frank knew it. "Think you could fix 'em?"

"I could try. Do we want to do this kind of music?"

Frank considered that. "Amy might sing it," he suggested.

"Now there's an idea. Let's work on it."

By dinner time, it still sucked but not as badly.

"I'm going to ask for Tiffany's input," I informed Frank. "I'll e-mail her the lyrics right after we eat."

"Should we ask her to come tomorrow?"

"If she wants to, I guess. We should let her know she's welcome."

Frank agreed. "Yeah, that would be the right thing to do."

~

Tiffany slipped me a note when she got on the bus. Since it was addressed "Martin and Frank," I held it where we both could read.

"I know you don't have time to check e-mail in the morning," it read, "so I'm writing this out to make certain it is what I want to say. I won't come this afternoon because it might influence you when you make a decision. If Peale isn't the right person, I'll try to play drums. If he joins, I can do something else, if you still want me." It was signed, simply, "Tiffany."

There was a P.S., however: "Check your e-mail for my ideas on your song. The chords sound good but I had to make up my own melody. I'm sure it's completely different from yours."

I looked back to Tiffany and nodded her an okay.

Chapter 24

Jimi looked nothing like his sister. She was all angles and elbows, long bones and jutting jaw. He was round-faced and soft.

I let him take my normal seat, next to Frank, and went back to sit near Amy and Tiffany. Tiff had filled Amy in on Jimi.

"Hey," I said to Tiffany, "I'll look at your e-mail as soon as I get home."

"Don't," she replied. "I kept coming up with new ideas all day. Wait until evening, okay?"

"For the revised version? Sure."

"You'll have to show it to me," Amy told her. "I'll come over."

"Uh-huh. Look at this." She had a music catalog. "Marlon told me about it."

She was pointing to music-writing software. "I checked my keyboard and I can hook it right up to the computer." She looked up. "If I buy a cable."

"And print it all out when you're done? That is neat." I had never paid any attention to this kind of music-making.

"It doesn't cost much," Tiffany added. "At least, the simpler versions."

"Some of them let you record sound, too."

"We wouldn't need that." I noted the "we." "Though Amy would probably love it." She smiled at her friend.

I told Amy, "It looks like this whole band thing is a go. If you want to sing with us, it's okay with me. You wouldn't mind, would you, Tiff?"

"Not at all. But how about them?" She nodded toward Jimi and Frank.

I took a look at the two. They'd been talking steadily since getting on. Robby was occasionally edging in a word.

"No problem. They'll take any chance they can get to play. I wish there was some way to involve Rob."

"Roadie," laughed Amy.

"Yeah, I'll tell him you suggested it. Hey, you know I meant that we could back you up, right?" She might have misunderstood. "Not make you our full-time vocalist. Though," I went on, "we may need one."

I couldn't tell if she was disappointed. "Oh," she said, "so, it would be, like, me performing solo, not as part of—have you decided what to call your band?"

"Not yet. If Jimi joins, we can go ahead and choose something. But, yeah, that was the idea; we could be your anonymous back-up band when you do the country thing."

"How do you like 'Betty Noir?'" Tiff abruptly asked.

"Who?"

"'Betty Noir,' as a name for the band."

"Oh, I get it." I gave her a pained smile. "But Frank wouldn't. He'd want to know which of us was Betty." I looked at Amy. "Are you in on the joke?"

"Tiff already explained it to me. It's French for the bogey-man or something like that." She turned to her friend. "No one else is going to get it, you know."

"It wouldn't matter, as long as we do," answered Tiffany.

Billie Peale hadn't lied; her brother could really play. I was the questionable one, as the bass player. Jimi and I had to be able to play together, in time. But that's what practice is for.

We didn't spend much time playing. Mostly, we just goofed off, showing Jimi around, talking about this and that. Frank dug into my folks' record collection (they still had some vinyl along with their CDs) and played a few things. He'd discovered punk-rock.

Jimi's sister came to pick him up after dinner, driving an ancient full-size sedan. It was older than she was.

As Jimi gathered his things to leave, Frank turned to me and asked, "Well, is he in?"

"Shouldn't we have a secret vote?" I innocently inquired.

Jimi thought I was serious but Frank knew better.

"Okay," I said, "Jimi's in, as far as I go. And I know you want him to join." Frank nodded. "So, if you want it," I told the drummer, "I guess you're part of the band. Provided," I wanted to make sure they understood, "Tiffany agrees."

"You know she will," said Frank.

"Yeah, but she's in on this so we have to actually ask her. You wouldn't want us to ignore *your* opinion."

Frank gave me a look but didn't say anything. I probably did ignore his opinions, sometimes.

"Are they any good?" Billie asked her brother.

"Martin has trouble keeping time," Jimi responded.

"Oh, I know that. I sit next to him in band."

"I'm not used to playing at a steady speed on my classical," I offered as an explanation, "or with other musicians."

"Good excuse," came Billie's dry comment.

Jimi laughed. "He can really play that guitar," he told Billie, "and he uses all his fingers!" I guess I'd impressed him. He'd impressed me, too.

"I'd heard that you played. Marlon mentioned it." She smiled at my expression. "Yeah, we talk about you behind your back."

~

"I'd never met Jimi's sister, before," said Frank. "She's kinda—different."

"Different good or different bad?" I'd just sat down at the computer.

"Different *different*," he laughed. "And I'm not sure whether she's really ugly or really good looking."

"She does have strong features."

Frank agreed. "That's it. She doesn't look, well, feminine." He paused. "But she still looks sexy."

"Feminine?" I asked. "I wouldn't mistake her for a guy."

"She's not curvy, like Amy. You know what I mean."

"Yeah, you think girls should be like marshmallows—soft and sweet," I teased him. "I thought you'd picked up more political correctness around my family."

"Not me. Checking your e-mail?"

"Uh-huh. Two messages here from Tiff. One from last night, one from this afternoon. Song revisions."

"That's a good change," he said, pointing at the screen.

"I don't know. A little too dramatic, isn't it?" I moved on to the later version. "I think this is better."

"Remember, it's for Amy," Frank reminded me.

"Right. Something that seems overblown to me might just suit her." I turned to face him. "You wouldn't mind playing back-up for her, would you? At the talent show, or whatever?"

"Naw, not as long as we do our stuff, too."

"Okay." I was feeling pretty good. "I think this may actually work out. But right now," I continued, "I have homework."

"Me, too," said Frank.

~

"My dad would like you to come fishing again, sometime," I told Robby. "Frank and I aren't enthusiastic enough for him."

"And you never come to the Lodge, anymore," added Frank.

"You two are always busy with this music stuff," he answered, "or working. I end up sitting around watching you."

"We don't have to do anything," I said.

"Yeah, we can just goof off," Frank continued. "Play video games or something."

"Watch a movie," I suggested.

"Invite beautiful women over," said Frank. We looked at him. "It's worth a try."

"The only beautiful women I'll see at your place are on video," Robby told him.

"I think you just insulted my mom," I responded, "but you're welcome, anyway."

"Will you be spending Thanksgiving in the woods?" asked Frank.

"We'll go out Friday and stay the rest of the weekend. Last time this season."

"Maybe in December, then," I said. "I mean, to go fishing."

"Yeah, maybe."

Frank didn't think that was soon enough. "But you can come home with us any afternoon."

"Okay," Robby laughed, "don't nag me, Frank. We'll do something." He thought a moment. "Next Wednesday," he decided, "if my parents say it's all right."

"The day before Thanksgiving?"

"The perfect time for it," I observed. "No school the next day, no homework, no worries."

"Exactly," agreed Rob.

"Can you stay overnight?" asked Frank.

"I suppose so." Robby looked at me. "Would your parents mind?"

"No. It'll be kind of cramped," I told him. "You've seen our room."

"I'll bring my sleeping bag. I can put it anywhere."

~

"So, your band is going to be in the talent show?" asked Marlon.

"We're aiming for it," I answered, "either backing Amy or on our own."

"No reason you can't do both."

"You think they'd let us?"

"Well, it's two different acts, isn't it? For that matter, you could do a solo spot, too," he told me, "assuming you pass the audition."

Suddenly suspicious, I looked at him. "You're on the committee," I accused.

He gave me an innocent smile. "Of course."

"Should I slip you a bribe?"

"Wouldn't hurt." He veered to another subject. "Are you ready for the concert? Your flute playing up to snuff?"

That would be the last week before Christmas vacation; one afternoon show for the school and an evening concert for the

119

public. Marlon was one of the students who would get a chance to conduct.

"I manage, and Billie's more than good enough to cover my short-comings on flute."

"Uh-huh. That piece from the 'Nutcracker' requires some good playing," he pointed out. "I know you're talented but do you practice enough? With all that other stuff you're into?"

"You're one to talk! But I try to fit it in. I don't particularly need to work on my reading or time, like some of these kids. Mainly, it's polishing my technique. Well, maybe my time, a little." I remembered what Billie had said.

"A lot of them will never be able to play very well, I suppose," admitted Marlon. "But *you* shouldn't slack off because of that."

"Yeah, I know. I do consider guitar my first instrument, though. It gets priority."

"Then you should certainly play it in the talent show. Do you do any styles besides strict classical? Like, jazz or anything?"

"I've fooled around with the folk thing," I said, "but not tunes so much as accompaniment."

"You mean, for singing?"

"Yeah, but there is absolutely, positively, emphatically no way I would sing at the show."

Chapter 25

"The deadline's coming for the next *Pine Tree*," Tiffany said. "Will you submit anything?"

"I think everyone liked your poem in the last issue," Amy told me, "but no one understood yours," she said to Tiff. "And don't tell me you don't care. If you didn't, you wouldn't let it be printed in the first place." She seemed pleased with her logic.

Tiff shrugged. "It would be nice if they did understand it but if they don't—they don't!"

"You can lead a horse to water but you can't make it read poetry," I observed.

"I couldn't have put it better," agreed Tiffany.

"You two are so weird, sometimes. Don't you want people to like your poems?"

"Sure, but if we changed one just so somebody would like it, it wouldn't be *our* poem, anymore." I looked at Tiff. "That makes sense, doesn't it?"

She nodded. I think I'd actually impressed her, for once. It was her kind of attitude.

"Has Marlon been asking for stuff?" I continued. "I have to admit, I haven't written much, lately."

"He's dropped hints," said Tiffany. "Don't you have some older thing you could turn in?"

"I guess so."

"Tiff's been doing a lot of writing," Amy reported.

"I know. She e-mails me some of it."

"Really?" She turned to her friend. "I'm amazed."

"It's—easier," Tiffany explained, "Easier than in person."

"Much easier," I agreed. "Anyway, while Marlon's on my mind—" I wasn't sure how to put this, so I just blurted it out. "Is he still against having Frank over here?" He'd said nothing more about it.

"Is that why Frank isn't with you?" asked Amy.

"Pretty much," I answered. This was my second visit to the Theos's house.

Tiff's dark eyebrows formed an angry vee. "Marlon told you not to bring Frank?"

"This was months ago," I told her. "I wasn't sure what your parents thought of him, either."

Amy was disapproving. "You should treat Frank better than that."

"Yeah, I know, but it never came up before. Neither of us was coming over."

Tiffany walked out of the room. Amy and I went to the door and watched her go into her father's office. When she came out, she simply said, "Frank will be over in a few minutes."

"A miracle!" exclaimed Amy. "Now she's calling up boys!"

~

"Could you play this?" asked Billie.

I looked it over. "Which part?" I asked, giving her my very best mischievous smile.

"Like you could handle the flute," she retorted. "That's mine."

"The second part was for classical guitar. "Yeah," I said, "I can do this. Where'd it come from?"

"Mr. Montero found it for me. There's extra credit if we'll work on it."

I gave her a look. "I smell a conspiracy."

"Who, me?" She flashed a broad, self-satisfied grin.

"And Marlon, no doubt. You two can talk Montero into anything." It was true; they were favorites.

"Okay, I confess. But will you do it?"

"Sure, it looks interesting." And short. "Hey, don't I get a solo?"

"This is *my* showpiece," she informed me. "You haven't paid your dues yet."

"Yes, ma'am, I'll remember my place. I can start working up my part as soon as I get home. The fingerings are shown," I pointed to a line of tablature, "so I won't have to take time figuring them out."

"We'll have to practice together. Mr. Montero says we can have some class time."

"And we could work during lunch," I suggested. "I'll have to start bringing my guitar to school."

"The practice rooms are usually open after school," said Billie. "We might try that. I could give you a ride home."

"That's out of your way."

"I'll be running Jimi back and forth."

~

The Theos had just had one of those really large-screen TVs delivered. "It's huge," Amy told us. "Like going to the movies." Then, she more-or-less invited us to Tiffany's house to watch. Tiff didn't mind, of course. That's what Amy did.

"You could bring some movies," Tiffany had suggested.

Amy added "Nothing that will shock her parents."

So, Friday afternoon, Frank and I pedaled over to the Theos's house. He was carrying the wide-screen version of "It's a Mad, Mad, Mad, Mad World." It was one of his favorite movies.

Marlon met us at the door. He didn't seem bothered by Frank's presence. "Come in, guys," he said. "Amy isn't with you?"

I shook my head. "I didn't know you'd be home," I told him.

"No game, tonight, and no plans." He grimaced. "So I'm baby-sitting."

Frank didn't get it right away but I did. "Your parents going out or something?"

"Yeah."

"Oh," said Frank, "*we're* the babies."

I laughed. "And Marlon has to be the responsible adult. Don't you get tired of that?"

"Comes naturally. Hey, Tiff," he called, "your dates are here."

She entered the room, holding a phone. "Amy's on her way over," she said, ignoring Marlon's gibe, "but she's bringing someone with her." She was clearly not happy about it.

"One of her red-neck boyfriends?" asked Marlon.

Tiffany nodded.

Frank nudged me. "Did you notice? Tiff's different tonight."

"Huh?" I looked at her. "No glasses!"

"Looking good," commented Frank.

I think Tiffany blushed; it doesn't really show on her. "Tiff always refused to wear contacts, before," said Marlon. "I don't know why."

Because *you* wear them, I thought. "She looked good all along," I informed Frank. "Don't pretend you never noticed."

~

Amy rode up a few minutes later, on the back of Earl Johnson's dirt bike. That was illegal but no one worried about it in Ruby.

If Frank and Marlon had one thing in common, it was dislike for the Johnson boy. In an odd way, it brought them closer together. Earl was my age but I didn't know him very well. I did know he sometimes hung around with J.R.

Tiffany took charge of the entertainment. She loaded the DVD player and then sat on the carpet with Frank and me. Marlon wandered in and out a few times, before settling in a chair with a bowl of popcorn.

"Couldn't you find anything new?" complained Earl, as the movie started. Amy hushed him. She wasn't acting like her normal self, at all. She was more subdued, more passive.

We watched Smiler Grogan's car go flying off the highway. "Hey," Frank said to Tiffany and me, "how about 'Smiler Grogan' as a band name?"

Tiff made a face. "It's no worse than 'Betty Noir,'" he told her.

"This is boring," said Earl. "Let's go somewhere else, Amy."

Frank and I tried to mind our own business but, from the corner of my eye, I could see Tiff give him a dirty look. I'd bet anything Marlon did, too.

But Amy just shrugged and acquiesced. "Sorry, Tiff," she said. "I'll call you later."

"That guy really burns me up," said Marlon, after they left.

"He's so rude," Tiffany stated, "and thinks he's the center of the world."

"Jocks." Marlon made the word sound distasteful.

Frank spoke up. "J.R.'s not like that."

"Oh, sure, you're right." Marlon looked at him. "I guess I've made some wrong judgments about you, too."

"I've been a good influence on him," I claimed.

"Okay, let's watch the movie," Frank suggested. We were making him uncomfortable. "I don't know what kind of excitement they'll find in Ruby, anyway."

"Yeah," I agreed. "It's really the middle of nowhere."

Frank gave me a look. I gave him one back. The same thought had struck us both. "That's *it*," he said. I nodded.

Tiffany was puzzled. "What are you talking about?"

"The name for our band," I announced, "is 'The Middle of Nowhere.'"

Chapter 26

It was our first "official" rehearsal.

"Frank should be front and center," I maintained, "'cause he's the cute one."

He thought I was kidding. "Martin's right," said Tiffany. "You'll make all the girls' hearts go pitter-patter."

"You're a god, man," I told him, "but don't let it go to your head."

Frank was the epitome of cute. Tall, long blonde hair, regular-but-boyish features, the whole package. He didn't even have zits.

"The singer should be in center," he protested.

"What singer?" Tiff and I asked simultaneously.

"Somebody has to sing." Frank looked at Jimi. "How's your voice?"

Jimi started in on a pop song we all knew. "He's no worse than the rest of us," I decided, "and he's willing."

The drummer shook his head. "I can't play and sing at the same time. It just don't work."

We were set up in the restaurant. Billie Peale had brought her brother by around noontime on Saturday, with his drum set in her back seat.

"Can you play a surf beat?" I asked him.

"I dunno. How's it go?"

Tiff demonstrated on the keyboard. "Aw, that's simple," said Jimi.

"Keep it that way," I begged. "We get confused easily."

"You wanta try 'Walk, Don't Run?'" inquired Frank. "We don't have a part for Tiff."

"I think an organ might fill out the arrangement, some. It sounds sparse when you're on lead guitar."

"Should I just play chords?" asked Tiffany, looking at her sheet.

"For now, yeah. That all right?" She nodded. "How about you, Frank?" I wasn't going to make decisions without asking even if they did sort of look at me as 'leader.'

"Let's do it," he said.

We got about four bars before Frank and Tiff fell out. "Hold it, Jimi," I called. "We've lost them."

"I thought *you* were the one who had problems with time."

"We just need to get used to playing together. Let Frank and me start it out and then you guys come in."

Jimi picked up our tempo. When we finished, he said "I should have a drum solo."

"That's only fair. We have solos," Frank pointed out.

I agreed. "And this is the piece for it. But not too long," I told them. "How about Tiff?"

"I don't need one," she was quick to answer.

"She can play a clarinet solo," joked Frank.

"Maybe we could just get rid of the guitarist and be a jazz trio," Tiffany retorted. "Clarinet, bass and drums."

"I like it," said Jimi.

"Right now, we should learn this song," I reminded them.

By the end of the afternoon, we had.

~

"Do you know what kind of health insurance your mother has?" Mom asked.

"None, I think," Frank answered. "She always took me to the free clinic."

Dad nodded, like he suspected as much. "Can we list him on ours? Or," he smiled, "should we try to pass him off as Jeff?" The intricacies of insurance policies were beyond my father.

"It shouldn't be a problem," Mom told him.

Frank was getting uneasy. "You don't need to do that. I—I can take care of myself."

"Sure," I said. "You gonna run off again to busk on some street corner?"

"Only if you come along to play accompaniment."

"If I have to, I will." I felt silly but I said it: "You're the best friend I've ever had."

127

"Oh, gee," He looked at Mom and Dad. "What's with Martin?"

I lightened it up. "Hey, man, don't worry. I'm not going to put my arm around you in public, or anything."

"You'd better not," he threatened, but with a grin.

"Ha, you don't scare me." I laughed. "You don't scare *anybody*."

"So you're a tough guy?" Frank asked. "Why don't you go teach Earl Johnson a lesson?"

"Me? You've gotta be kidding. You're bigger; you do it."

"He's already beaten me up too many times."

"Really?" asked Mom. "When was this?"

"Every now and then since I was little," Frank responded. "Once, I was stupid enough to call him 'Earl the Girl.'" He gave us an embarrassed smile. "Earl's beaten up just about everyone at some time. I remember when he punched Marlon. Broke his glasses—and his nose. That was, like, four or five years ago."

"No wonder you two dislike him," I observed.

"We're not the only ones," he assured me.

~

Mr. Montero had never heard me on guitar, so I had to run through some things for him.

He nodded when I was done. "I assumed you could play. That's why I okayed Billie's idea." He looked over to her, seated in the corner. "Did you explain the whole deal?"

"Not yet." I squinted questions in her direction but she ignored me.

"You'd better; this is your project," Mr. Montero told her. He was always very earnest and always willing to take people at their word. Naturally, some took advantage of that but the core of serious students was very loyal to him.

"Yes, sir," she replied.

He left us in our small practice room. "What's the 'whole deal?'" I inquired.

"We'll get credit just for learning the piece and playing it in class." I nodded; I'd understood that. "But we'll get more credit if we're in the talent show." She held up her hand to keep me from speaking. "Montero likes his students to perform in public. Wants to show us off, I guess."

I considered that. "Oh, well," I said, "I intend to be there, anyway."

"Yeah, your band. I appreciate you taking on Jimi."

"We're lucky to have him. And it's Frank's doing."

"Sure. Let's try running through it."

We were pretty ragged but we managed the whole piece without stopping. When we finished, Billie stated, "You've already memorized it."

"Well, yes. Haven't you?" I tried but I couldn't keep a straight face. "I'm used to doing it. My part's pretty easy, too.

"You think so?"

"Yeah, really. It's mostly repeated patterns," I pointed out, "and I have a little leeway where it gets too difficult. No one will notice if I simplify, a tad."

She laughed. "Oh, you're cheating?"

"My hands aren't big enough to play everything the way it's written."

"Hmm. Okay, you're the expert. Let's go again."

～

"It looks like you're already filling up," noted Robby.

"Every room should be occupied tonight," my dad told him.

"But that doesn't mean we'll be too busy to do anything," I added. "I'll be working in the morning but not today."

"How about Frank? Will he have any free time, tomorrow?" Frank had declined to ride out to the Dells' house with us.

Dad spoke. "He may have to help a little, since Amy's not coming."

"Yeah, but if you sleep in, you'll hardly notice."

"Good idea. Amy won't be here?" he asked. I think he may have been a bit disappointed.

129

"Not tomorrow," I said. "She's doing something with her family."

"Oh, probably at the church. Pastor Fred hasn't been happy about her missing Sundays."

We walked into the restaurant. "Amy reminds me of her Uncle Fred," said Dad. "The way they talk."

"And talk and talk," I continued. "Frank must be upstairs."

"No, he's in my office," Mom let us know, "using the computer." Her "office" was a former storeroom, off the kitchen. We sometimes used her computer, which was newer and faster than mine.

"Whatcha doing?" Rob asked him.

"Downloading games. And other stuff."

"If you download a virus, Mom will murder you." I looked at some things he'd printed out. "Public records?"

"I've been looking up people I know, but there isn't much info."

"A lot of it may never have been put into computers," I guessed.

He nodded. "The only thing I could find on Bill was a business license, and it's expired."

"How'd you learn to do this?" Rob was mystified.

Frank held out a book. "Marlon lent it to me."

I turned to Robby. "Now there's a friendship I never expected to see."

"Um, isn't Marlon, well, you know—" Robby couldn't find appropriate words but he did make a gesture.

"You're kidding," said Frank. He looked from one of us to the other. "Oh, so what?" He shrugged. "Marlon's still okay."

"Rob's just guessing, anyway."

"Yeah," he admitted, "but you have to admit he doesn't act very masculine."

"That doesn't mean anything," I replied. "We don't all have to be Mr. Macho."

"You're proof of that," snickered Frank. "Hey, Billie's going to be disappointed. I mean, if you're right," he said to Rob.

"She does like him," I agreed, "but seems reluctant to do anything about it."

"Billie Peale?" Robby whistled. "And Marlon? Boy, what a combination."

Chapter 27

It was good to be able to spend some time with Robby. My other friends were a little less down-to-earth than he; shoot, they all seemed to float a few feet above the ground.

We didn't really do anything. We tried out the new games Frank had found but they weren't as good as the ones we already had. Then we watched a couple of movies. Frank and Rob were better at staying up late so I don't remember much of the second one.

The next day, Thanksgiving, they hung around on the docks until Rob's father came to pick him up. I was busy in the restaurant, first, then doing up rooms. Frank had helped early, when there was a crowd.

"Are you sure your mom's expecting me?" I asked, as we cleaned up.

"Yeah, man, don't worry," he reassured me.

"If there are only four plates on the table, you're in big trouble," I warned.

We went down to get our bikes.

"I'll be glad when you start driving," Frank told me. Robby and I could both get our licenses in the spring.

"I'm allowed to operate a moped, right now," I reminded him. "Should I campaign for one at Christmas?"

"That might be—" A light bulb went on over his head. "Tell your folks to buy some for rentals. Then we could use them."

"You are one devious kid," I remarked.

"You said you'd been an influence on me."

"Sure, blame me," I complained. "But, hey, do let me be an influence on you today: play it cool, okay?"

"I didn't intend to start a fight or anything." He sounded peeved. "Sometimes, you act like I'm an idiot."

"I just mean no smart remarks and don't let things bug you," I advised him. "And you *are* an idiot."

My bike is better than Frank's little banana-seat model; he couldn't catch me before we reached his mom's.

~

"We need a dart gun," I whispered to Frank. "My brother uses one to shoot roaches in his dorm."

We were watching one of the dark, wide-body variety climb the wall. Around here, they call them "palmetto bugs."

"That kind doesn't hurt nothin'," yawned Bill. "Just wandered in from outdoors."

"They stink when you smash 'em," added Jason.

"Shouldn't you be helpin' your mother?" Bill asked him.

"We'll do that," I volunteered. "Come on, Frank." I couldn't take any more football.

Frank's mom was no more a cook than mine. I mean, either one could put a meal on the table but it was just a chore for them. That's why Dad was fixing the feast, back at the Lodge.

For Ms. Differs, it was stuffing-in-a-box, cranberries-in-a-can, frozen vegetables and whatever else was quick and easy. Nothing's wrong with that; if you don't like to cook, why spend a lot of time on it?

"Need any help, Mom?" asked Frank from the kitchen doorway.

"The turkey should come out in a few minutes," she told us. "If you can take care of that, I won't have to call Bill in." Ms. Differs wasn't capable of lifting it herself. "Then, you could go ahead and set the table." She looked at me. "Do you drink tea, Martin?"

"Yes, ma'am," I replied. "Sweet."

A faint smile passed across her face. "A southern boy. I'll make up a pitcher." Frank wasn't much on iced tea but he kept his mouth shut. After all, his mother knew that.

We hoisted the turkey out, one on each end of the roasting pan, and onto a platter. It would have to sit awhile before Bill could carve, so we went to set the table.

"You mind sitting next to Jason?" Frank asked. "I want to be by my mom."

"I'll survive," I answered. "Everyone get these big glasses?"

"Yeah. We don't have fancy goblets, like at your place."

"Then how do you serve the champagne?"

"And you tell *me* not to make smart remarks!"

"Sorry," I apologized. "I'll be good. Seriously, everyone's drinking tea?"

"I'm gonna grab a soda, but yeah," he added, in a low voice, "Mom won't allow alcohol in the house."

~

"You ate too much, man. You'll never make it back to the Lodge."

"You're the one who barfs," Frank reminded me. "Let's take our time."

We pedaled slowly along. "That went okay," I remarked.

"Yeah," he grunted. "Here comes a hill."

"Is that what you call this little bump?" Shifting down a gear, I looked over at him. "Can you handle it?"

"I'd—better walk it up." Frank's bike was single speed.

We both dismounted. "Think you'll want another dinner?" I asked, as we reached the top.

He gave me a weak smile. "How soon?"

"At least an hour and a half, maybe two. I know you. You'll be hungry by then."

He nodded, sort of absentmindedly. "Thanks for coming with me."

"Well, thanks for having me, Mr. Hanley. We can coast, now."

We glided down the other side of what passes for a hill in Ruby. It was a long, shallow grade, shallow enough that we occasionally had to pedal.

"I'm feeling better now," reported Frank. "What's for dessert?"

"Pumpkin pecan pie, of course. But you'll want some of Dad's dressing, too, and homemade cranberry compote."

"That gunk you were mixing up? Smelled more like com*post*."

"You won't say that when you taste it. It's way better than the canned stuff. Not to disrespect your mom's cooking or anything."

Frank had to laugh at that. "I know she can't cook. She knows she can't cook."

"She doesn't have to; she looks good." I don't know why I said that.

He gave me a very strange look. "You think so, too?"

"Sure. She's almost as pretty as you."

~

Frank didn't disappoint me; he managed to down another dinner, with ease. He even took a second piece of pie.

As we were clearing the table, Frank whispered to me "Your folks drank a lot of wine."

"They didn't even finish the bottle," I pointed out, "though they came closer than usual." I sloshed the remnant around. Mom and Dad weren't much in the way of drinkers. Some wine on holidays or with Sunday dinner was it.

"Did you ever try any?" he asked.

"They've let me taste a sip. I didn't think much of it."

"Mom says I should never drink," Frank told me. "Alcoholism runs in the family."

"Oh?" I thought about it for a moment. "None of my relatives have that problem. None that I know of. Maybe there's an uncle locked away somewhere." He barely noticed the joke. "Our doctor back in Atlanta said I probably shouldn't drink wine 'cause it can set off migraines. Especially the red."

"I read somewhere that red wine's good for you."

"My folks like to think so."

Frank laughed at that one. "I guess we'd both better avoid it. I don't want to end up attending AA meetings with my mom." He looked up at the clock. "Almost time for wrestling. Let's get the rest of this cleared away.

"And Martin?" he added, with just a trace of adolescent embarrassment. "Thanks. Thanks for Thanksgiving."

"Sure, man. That's what the day is for, isn't it?"

Chapter 28

"I'm the one who should have a moped," declared Amy, "so I won't need a ride over here."

Frank had mentioned his idea to her. "Have you saved enough money?"

"Yes, but I have other plans for it." She wouldn't tell us more.

Amy made plenty, just from tips, working three holiday mornings. We had big crowds on Friday and Saturday: people who came for a day of fishing and went home again in the evening.

That Sunday, Jason came over and Dad took him and Frank out onto the river for a couple of hours.

"Use him for bait," I recommended, but the brat came back in one piece. By that time, most guests had checked out.

I was vacuuming when Frank came in. "Gonna do any more rooms today?" he asked.

"Naw. Six is enough." That took nearly a full afternoon. "How'd the fishing go?"

"We hooked a few trout. I helped Jason clean them to take home."

"Check for worms?" It's a problem with trout.

"Yeah, they were okay." He grinned. "You know, once they're cooked, you can't tell the worms from the fish."

"Blech. I'll bet Dad told you that."

He nodded. "He says they're just as safe to eat as the trout."

"I suppose. One more unit to vacuum." I preferred to clean by the task rather than by the room. "Maybe we can take Robby fishing, soon. I know he'd like to go after some trout."

"I wonder if Jimi likes to fish," said Frank.

"When we get him here, we'd better keep him busy practicing," I recommended. "We should try practicing with Amy, too."

"Does she like the song?"

"I guess, but she heard it with Tiff's melody. We'll have to straighten that out, also."

~

"Have you been working out?" I asked Robby. "You look bigger." I'd been noticing it for a while.

"Uh-huh. We had a set of weights rusting away so I started using them. J.R. showed me some lifts."

"I wish I gained that easily."

"He's getting big and strong so he can carry our equipment," Frank decided. We'd told him of Amy's "roadie" concept.

"Or, he could do security and protect us from crazed fans."

"More likely, keep 'em from throwing tomatoes," Robby stated.

"You are welcome at rehearsals," I let him know, "if you don't think you'd be bored."

"When are we going fishing?" asked Frank.

"How about the weekend after next?" suggested Robby, "and let's invite J.R. this time."

"Okay," said Frank. He was willing to accommodate Rob. I nodded my agreement.

"Amy's not at her stop," noted Frank, as we drove by.

"Probably at Tiff's," I said, but she wasn't.

~

"She could have phoned me," complained Tiffany. "I didn't know where she was, either." Amy had chosen, at the last moment, to accept a ride to school.

"How about this afternoon? We should get together."

"She promised to come by. Can you make it?"

"I have some work but if Frank helps we can be over by five."

"That's fine. I have a couple of things to, uh, discuss."

As usual, Tiff was hard to read. "Oh, no," I gasped, "you're kicking me out of the band. I've seen it coming!"

"Don't give me ideas." She did smile. "I suppose Billie is waiting impatiently."

"I'm not hurrying lunch for her," I declared. "I don't think she and Mr. Montero realize how hard it will be to hear my guitar on stage."

"You'd be louder if you used your fingernails, right?"

"Yes, but it's a little late to change my technique. It would mess up my bass playing, too."

"I thought it already was—well, let's not go there."

I laughed. "Good idea."

"Can't you use a microphone?"

"May have to. It's hard to set up right, I guess, even if you know what you're doing." I was unsure about mentioning a solo number but I knew I'd have to tell Tiff, and the others, sooner or later. "If I did a piece by myself, amplification wouldn't be as important."

"Marlon said you might." Her smile hinted of smugness. "I was wondering when you'd bring it up."

"I haven't even decided yet," I said in my defense.

"Would you learn something new?"

"No time for that; not with all these other things going on. I played a piece in my last recital that might work."

"Not Bach, I hope. It would put everyone to sleep."

"No, it's a folk song arrangement. Billie and I are doing Satie." She nodded knowingly. "'Gymnopedie Number One.'"

"Oh, that's pretty. Is it hard?"

"Easier than Bach."

~

"Come into Marlon's room," Amy told us. "Tiff's in there."

She was seated at the computer. "Listen," she said, and hit the space bar. Music began to play.

Tiffany leaned back and smiled. "Do you recognize it?"

"I can guess what it's supposed to be. Can't you?" I asked Frank.

"Our song?"

Amy spoke up. "She wouldn't let me tell you she'd ordered that software."

"Marlon and I spent the weekend and barely started to figure it out," Tiff admitted, "but this was fairly easy."

"Can we do it with my tune?" Frank wanted to know.

"Uh-huh. We'll just—copy it to a new file—okay, and then keep the chords and lyrics but delete the melody. There we are; now we can put in a new tune."

It took awhile; we'd hunt around on the keyboard to find the notes and then enter them, one by one, with the mouse.

"If we knew the melody well enough," Tiffany explained, "we could just play it in."

Marlon came in while we were busy. "That's pretty neat, huh? But you'd better wind it up."

"Oh." Tiffany checked the time. "You can lose track." She looked at us. "Do you think—?" She turned to Marlon.

"Better not," he warned. "Not three uninvited dinner guests." Sibling telepathy; Jeff and I have it, too.

"Some other time," I suggested. "It's getting pretty dark out."

"I'll print out what we've got so far," decided Tiffany. "Then you can pencil in the rest of your tune. Um, do you remember how to set it up, Marlon?"

They fiddled with it a bit and the printer started. Marlon looked at the first sheet. "I guess we did it correctly," he reported.

"Here," Tiff said, and handed us some pages. "I already printed out my version."

"You should install the program in your computer," Marlon told me. "Then you could swap files."

"Martin's PC is old and slow. Has a lousy sound-card, too," Frank said.

I shrugged. "I might try it. If mine's inadequate, I could use my parents'."

"Jimi's coming tomorrow?" Tiffany didn't wait for an answer. "Why don't we rehearse over here? We can set up downstairs where there's lots of room."

"Don't worry," added Marlon, "she's already cleared it with the parental units."

"Sounds okay to me," I responded.

Frank wasn't sure. "What about transportation?"

"I think I have that covered."

Chapter 29

"Do you mind if Jimi stays?"

"As long as he doesn't start drumming," I stipulated.

"I'll just do my homework," he promised. "She won't take me unless I finish it."

"Let's begin." Billie started the metronome.

"Wait. I need to tune first." She'd forgotten about that. Classical guitars always seem to be out of tune.

We practiced for twenty minutes or so, working to get our timing tight. I hate metronomes.

"All done," said Jimi.

"They don't give you enough homework," I told him. "How about one more time through," I suggested to Billie, "without the tick-tock?"

This was the first time we'd tried practicing after school. We finished half an hour of work and then went to get Jimi's drums.

The Peales lived in a rather run-down looking neighborhood that was actually only a couple of blocks from the school, if one walked. It was more roundabout by car.

"You need new shocks," I told Billie, as we bounced through the potholes.

"What we need is a new street," she replied, "or better yet, a house on a different street. Here we are. Now be polite to Gramma. She wouldn't get those 'zingers' of yours."

The house was small, and old, but the yard was neat. It appeared that someone was into gardening (maybe "Gramma"), though the flower beds were empty now.

Her grandmother was an impressively tall woman, wearing thick glasses. I thought Billie resembled her quite a bit. She did seem confused about who I was. Apparently, she'd heard Billie speak frequently of Marlon. I'm not positive she ever got us completely straight in her mind.

We loaded Jimi's drums. They took up a lot of room, even in her huge back seat. Then, it was off to Ruby.

"Your sister likes to drive fast, doesn't she?" I asked Jimi. He was seated between us, up front.

"What was that?" shouted Billie, over the blaring radio. "You want me to drive faster?" She started accelerating and then laughed and returned to her cruising speed, well over the limit.

"She's crazy," Jimi confided. "It's the family secret."

~

I'd already worked it out with Billie. We stopped at the Lodge to pick up Frank and our equipment. Pretty much everything fitted into the trunk. I suggested stowing Frank there, too, but he wouldn't go for it.

"I don't know the way," Billie told me. "Only that it's by the river."

"Just continue on this road. I'll tell you when to stop."

"You've never gone to see Marlon?" queried Frank, from the back seat.

"He's never invited me."

"He's afraid of you," was Jimi's opinion. "We're all afraid of you."

I thought there might be too much truth in that for comfort, so I kept my mouth closed.

"Didn't you say it was close?" she asked, after a minute or two.

"It is if you use the shortcuts," said Frank.

"This road follows a wide curve," I explained, "but you can't get lost on it. Here we go."

"That big old barn? Kinda ugly, isn't it?"

"Yuppy chic," I laughed. "Just park in the driveway. It'll add some class to the place."

"Don't make fun of my wheels." She pulled in beside Mrs. Theo's mini-van.

Tiff and Amy were sitting at the bottom of the rear stairway. For once, Amy actually seemed a little bashful. I'd forgotten that she didn't know Billie.

"Hey, Amy," I said, "this is Billie Peale, our new roadie."

Billie ignored me and politely said "Hello" and "Pleased to meet you." Then she added, impishly, "Jimi told me you were cute."

That flustered Amy, not to mention Jimi, but Tiffany said, "Oh, all the boys think that."

"They're so shallow, aren't they?" asked Billie. She and Tiff laughed. In a moment, Amy started giggling, too.

Frank was impatient. "Let's unload."

As we were getting our equipment, Messy Parker's Mustang stopped to let Marlon out. He hadn't expected Billie's presence and, although they were friends, he seemed uncomfortable and a little cool.

For once, we could plug everything in without worrying about the wiring. And the day was warm, so it felt good to be semi-outdoors. We didn't play very loud; there were neighbors. You couldn't hear the little speakers in Tiff's keyboard, either, if Frank and I cranked our amps.

"When you play at school," Marlon pointed out, "she can plug into the PA."

We hadn't worked out our music yet. We were just fooling around, getting a feel for playing together. After a while, Marlon invited Billie upstairs to show her the place. Amy suggested that we "cover" a country song in addition to the one we were trying to write.

"Find us the music," I told her, "and we'll attempt it."

"Make it an easy key," added Frank.

"Amateur," I chided him.

As we wound down, Tiffany suggested "You could leave your amps. I'll lock them in there." She gestured toward a storage room by the stairs.

"If we keep practicing here—" Frank said.

"We might as well," I finished. "But it may get too cold." I slapped at something biting my arm. "The sand gnats are coming out."

Jimi spoke up. "I want my drums at home."

I nodded. "Yeah, let's load 'em up."

When we had everything stowed, we went upstairs to find Billie. She and Marlon were at the computer, oblivious to all else.

"Oh, we have to go," said Billie. "I'll see you tomorrow, Marlon."

~

"I hope you aren't letting your studies suffer," said Mom.

It was late; Frank had turned in, so I was finishing my homework downstairs.

"No, Mom, I'm keeping up. If anything's suffering, it's my other interests. I haven't painted at all."

"Your grades will be good, then?"

"I guess. I'm not having any major problems. But this is hard for me." I pushed the book away. "I'll never be an A student in algebra."

"You did so well in geometry."

"Remember Algebra I? It was Bs and Cs there, too," I reminded her. "This will fill my math requirement, you know. I don't think I'll take any more after this year." I'd been thinking about it for a while.

Mom didn't seem bothered by the idea. "I never saw you in a math or science career, anyway." She smiled. "I'm sure there will be *some* As on your next report."

"PE will bring my average down, again. I just don't have the attitude Coach Munn wants. I'm not a 'team player,' whatever that means."

Mom laughed out loud. "You are one of the least competitive, least team-oriented people I've ever seen."

"That's good, right?" I joked. I hoped it was.

"You make up for it by being a perfectionist," she answered. "That can drive someone to succeed just as much as being a competitor." She paused to think of an example. "Like the baseball player who's only reason for being on the team is to come in

145

to hit the long ball. He may be a terrible team player, he may not even care who wins, but he's worked on perfecting his home-run swing."

"Oh, I get it. Pitchers are a lot like that, too." A thought came to me. "It's almost an art-form to them."

Mom nodded. "I suppose it is. Though I was exaggerating; a successful athlete would need at least a bit of competitor in him."

"And a bit of perfectionist, too."

Chapter 30

"You did me a big favor."

"Always glad to oblige," I told Marlon. "What was it? By the way, that's Tiff's seat."

"She always sits opposite you?"

I nodded. Sometime, I'd just stopped going to the table where Marlon and his crowd ate lunch. Being on the edge of that group didn't have the appeal it once did.

"She'll make room for big brother, today," he announced. "We'll tell her I'm chaperoning. I've had my eye on you two!"

"You're the one who has to live with her," I warned him.

"Good point. Anyway, I want to thank you for bringing Billie over." He looked slightly embarrassed. "I was always, well, unsure about inviting her. Awkward. Not because she's black or anything," he hastened to tell me. "Because she's—Billie."

I probably understood better than Marlon realized. He'd been concerned about his image.

Tiffany came, carrying a tray. She gave Marlon a sour look but sat beside him without saying a word.

"Why don't you ever sit next to Martin?" he asked her.

She looked at me, so I tried to formulate an answer. "We need our space?"

Tiff smiled. "Sounds good."

"I think you just like making eyes at each other," said Marlon. "Oops, sorry." He held up his hands. "I should keep my mouth shut." Yeah, sure he was sorry.

I changed the subject. "So Billie's race wasn't a factor? I mean, it is Ruby."

"Well—you know Billie. If some red-neck made a remark to her, she'd belt him."

"And she's big enough to do some damage." I started to smile as a picture came to me. "It would be like that Conan movie. You know, the second one."

"The one that's not very good," commented Tiffany.

"Oh, I know what you mean," Marlon laughed. "What was that woman's name?"

None of us could remember.

The seats beyond us were filling. Somehow, Tiffany and I had attracted the "outcast" element to our table. It certainly wasn't anything we did. In fact, we hardly ever talked to them. Nonetheless, we were like the king and queen of "Loserville."

A rather heavy girl (I thought her name was Jodie) always tried to sit next to Tiff and listened to our every word. It was disconcerting at first. After awhile, I must admit, we hardly noticed her.

"Now the proverbial ice is broken, I think Billie will be coming around a lot," Marlon continued. "I should go to her house, sometime."

I laughed. "Boy is her Gramma going to be confused."

~

"Isn't that an Elvis song?" asked Frank.

"Sort of," I answered. "He did it with new words." I played a couple of bars. "It's called 'Aura Lee.'"

"Oh, I remember that from music class when I was in—Fourth Grade? Yeah." Then he thought again. "Or maybe Fifth. Folk music, huh?"

"Actually a pop song of its time, not a folk song," I told him. "It was popular during the Civil War."

"That what you're doing at the talent show?"

"Yeah. It's part of a medley I have here." I held out the music. "But the whole thing's kind of long. Maybe I'll just do one tune."

Frank looked it over. "I know 'Dixie.' How does 'The Rebel Soldier' go?"

I played some of it and then, for some reason, started singing.

"That's a sad one," commented Frank. "How come you know the words?"

"Ever seen a Civil War reenactment?"

He shook his head.

"I knew a kid in Atlanta who went to them. His whole family was into it."

"Did they dress up like soldiers?"

"Yeah, except his mom. She'd be a nurse. Anyway, they invited me along, once, and I heard a lot of these songs. That's why I dug the music up in the first place," I explained, "and 'The Rebel Soldier' just appealed to me."

"You like the sad stuff, don't you? You don't really seem happy, most of the time." Frank could be insightful.

"I guess not," I admitted. "That's just my personality."

"Sad?"

"My mom says I'm 'melancholy.' 'Sad' sounds like I go around crying!"

"You almost were on that song. Why don't you sing it in the show?"

"Never happen," I assured him.

~

"I thought *my* poems were depressing." Tiff sat at the lunch table, reading the new *Pine Tree*. "But this is something else."

"I was in a bad mood that day."

Unexpectedly, Tiffany's silent shadow spoke. "Would—you sign my copy?" She'd never said a word to me, before.

I was dumbfounded. "She's serious," Tiffany prompted, as I sat there like a lump.

"Oh—oh, sure." I took the magazine she held out. "J-O-D-I-E?"

She shook her head. "Y on the end, right?" asked Tiff.

"Yes." She built herself up to ask me a question. "Do you really feel that way?"

I made a wry face. "Sometimes," I confessed. "Therapy helps." She seemed to take me quite seriously. "That's a joke," I told her.

She smiled. "Th-thank you." Jody sat looking at my inscription for a few moments. Then, she abruptly got up and left.

"You'd better not laugh," I warned Tiff.

"I wouldn't think of it." She obviously was thinking of it but she only smiled a little. "She has a crush and a half on you."

"She's a girl and a half. No, don't say it, Tiff, I know that's unkind." I sighed. "I thought she was your disciple or something. You're the one she follows around."

"You know the cliché," Tiffany said. "'Misery loves company.' She's pretty miserable, I'd guess."

"And she thinks she's found a soul-mate." I looked down the table. "Misery seems to have a lot of company."

She laughed. "We're both getting depressed. Let's get out of here."

~

"Is this the key you want?" I asked Amy.

"I don't think so. Can you change it?"

Tiff's smile bordered on the condescending. "Yes, Amy," she said, "that's easy."

"Just start singing. We'll figure it out," I told her. After attempting to follow her on the keyboard, I reported "She's in F, I think."

Tiffany transposed it on the computer and Amy tried to sing along. "Too fast," she decided, "but the key's good."

"We can go up and down or faster and slower to fine tune it for you," Tiff let her know. "Otherwise, it's a finished product." We had cobbled together the definitive version of our song.

"Can you do that with anything?" Amy asked.

"Yeah," chimed in Frank. "We can even record it onto a cassette for you."

"You're kidding. I've been paying a lot for those back-up tapes." Amy looked disgusted. "And they are never just right for me."

"Did you pick another song?" inquired Tiffany.

"Uh-huh." Amy dug in her tote-bag. "Here it is." She opened a dog-eared songbook.

"A classic," I commented. "Let's try working it up on the computer."

"Let me do this one." Frank looked it over. "What's 'Western Swing?'"

"I'll assist you," I offered, "when we get home." We had installed Tiff's "sequencing" software on our computer. Well, Mom's actually.

"Can't you just learn it from the book?" Amy wanted to know.

"This way we can print out copies for everyone, in whatever key you choose," Tiff informed her. "Or, if you want, make you a back-up tape."

"You're—you don't have to go to so much trouble for me." Amy's voice seemed to break a little.

"We're your friends," Frank told her.

"I know," she replied, "I know," and she started sobbing.

"Go home," Tiff whispered, shooing us out the door.

Chapter 31

"What was all that about?"

"Beats me. *Something's* bothering her."

"If it's Earl, I'll—" Frank didn't know what he'd do.

"It's got to be more than that," I was certain, "but we aren't going to figure it out."

We pedaled on through the evening.

"You don't think we did anything, do you?" I wondered. I was thinking of all the times I'd been cool—too cool—toward Amy. "Maybe we should have asked her to join the band."

"I didn't think she'd want to".

"Neither did I."

"I dunno," said Frank, "maybe she does feel left out."

"She has other friends," I reminded him, "lots of them."

"But none as close as Tiffany."

I sighed. "Even Amy's gonna think life sucks, sometimes."

"Yeah," Frank agreed, "I guess she's pretty much like the rest of us."

"You have any homework?"

"I finished my math in English," he replied, "and my English in history. I can start right in on her music. After we eat."

~

Next morning felt awkward. Frank and I were concerned about Amy but didn't want to say anything that might embarrass her. We weren't even sure whether to bring in Robby.

"He might know something," Frank thought, "or he could talk to J.R."

"I don't find many chances to talk with Robby one-on-one," I said. "We never get to gossip about you behind your back."

"We do that to you all the time."

We didn't say anything to Rob on the bus but Frank intended to play detective at school. "I'll be subtle," he promised. I hoped so but subtlety was not Frank's forte.

Amy seemed her normal self, so we treated her that way. She

sat by Tiff and chatted with her girlfriends, the way she always did.

"Do you think Jimi could come over this weekend?" I asked Frank. We'd get more done."

"Billie will be busy. Marching band's going to some parade."

"Oh, yeah. Can't anyone else bring him?'

"His mom's going along as a chaperone and his father's working," said Frank. "He paints houses."

"So do I," I snickered, "in landscapes."

"Ha-ha."

"That ain't worth but one 'ha,'" Rob told us. Then he asked, "Why don't you go pick him up?"

"Because we're busy on Saturdays, too."

Frank commented, "It's a good thing the talent show is on a weeknight."

"What night is it?" I asked. "Let me check my calendar." I kept one in my binder.

"There." Frank pointed. "A Thursday."

Robby looked. "When are the auditions?"

"Earlier the same week," said Frank. "Monday and Tuesday, after school."

"You sure?"

"I remember the important things," he responded.

~

"She felt like an outsider—and a dummy"

"Can we do anything? Let's face it," I told Tiff, "we know fitting in can be hard, sometimes."

"Amy's never really faced that problem. If nothing else, she always had me—and I had her." Tiffany sounded frustrated and I knew I wasn't helping.

"So she's not prepared, huh? We have calluses." I was showing them, too, with that sort of comment.

"You have too many," she snapped.

I couldn't answer that. I looked at Tiff. I looked down.

"Oh, I shouldn't have said that." She was instantly apologetic. "I didn't mean to hurt you, too."

"It—only hurt 'cause it's true, I guess." And because it came from Tiff. I felt warm.

After a moment, I managed a smile. "You almost had another crier on your hands." I noticed Jody hanging on my words—my stupid, flippant words. "It's good for you," I told her. Then I looked around. "But not in front of the whole school."

Tiffany shook her head. "You're just as emotional as Amy, aren't you? But you've found a way to cover it up."

"It was just a little attack of self-pity. They pass. Uh-oh." I nodded toward Jody; *she'd* started to puddle up.

Tiffany regarded her, and then me. I shrugged. "We set her off, somehow."

For a few seconds, I thought Tiff might try to comfort the girl. Instead, she grabbed her tray and stood up. "This is too much. I'll see you in band," she declared, and left.

I gave a Jody a little smile. "Ah, alone at last," I kidded. She giggled through her tears.

"I—I'm sorry," she managed to get out.

"Yeah, we all are," I agreed, handing her a napkin. "Sorry for ourselves."

~

"What was wrong with her?" Tiff wanted to know.

"I think we're her favorite soap opera." She gave me a quizzical stare. "She identifies with us."

"She felt sorry for her poor, little, romantic poet?" Tiffany seemed to think that was amusing.

"It's like crying at a sad movie." I tipped my head. "But you don't do that, do you?"

"Never," she maintained, and then laughed. "I'm a regular warrior princess."

"You and Billie. Klingon women!"

"I like that," came Billie's voice from behind me. "It is a compliment, isn't it?"

"Absolutely. Ready to practice?"

"Naah, it's too nice to be cooped up in a little room. Let's sit outside."

"Why don't you bring your guitar?" asked Tiffany.

The Pinelands campus has lots of trees and open space. We found a shaded bench near the band room's back door.

"I don't think Atlanta ever gets this warm in December," I commented, as I tuned up.

"Play something," Billie demanded.

"Will you pass the hat when I'm done?" I launched into my Civil War medley.

"When you gonna sing?" she asked. "Jimi says you sing." She had her eyes closed and seemed half-asleep, lying on the grass.

Tiff became interested. "How would he know?"

"Motor-mouth Frank told him," I guessed. "Right?"

"Uh-huh. Hi, Marlon."

He was passing by on his way to the class room. "You know what would sound good with that?" he asked. "One of those Irish drums."

"Oh, whatcha call 'em, a bodhran?"

"Yeah, that's it."

"Martin's going to sing," Tiffany informed him.

Marlon raised an eyebrow.

"Your sister lies."

"Tiffany? I'm shocked."

"I put her up to it," Billie claimed.

"From you, I expect it," laughed Marlon. "I would like to hear you, sometime," he told me, "but I know this isn't the place. And the bell's about to ring."

~

Tiffany's room had mutated from Gothic to Punk. I blame Frank for that; he'd introduced her to the genre. I wasn't at all surprised that she also had found an affinity for my dad's Patti Smith records.

"Amy's busy again?" asked Frank.

Tiff nodded. "She's avoiding us, I'm sure."

"We can't back her," I pointed out, "if she won't practice with us."

"She did come over last night. We got both songs worked out well enough that she could use them on back-up tapes."

Frank was doubtful. "They sound so mechanical and they need a lead guitar or something to fill them out."

"We could add fills with the keyboard," I suggested. "Something simple."

"Can't we record my guitar, some way?"

"We'd need a mixer or something. And a better guitarist," I couldn't resist adding.

"Cut it out, Martin," Tiffany exploded. "Don't be so nasty."

Frank came to my defense. "Aw, he's just joking," he said. "It's Martin's thing."

"He does his thing too often. I'm sick of it."

For a moment, I was angry, but I have trouble staying that way. "Sorry, Tiff, it's my way of coping," I explained. "It's better than brooding."

I shouldn't have said that. Tiffany took it as criticism. "Well, brooding is what I do."

"Why are you two mad at each other?" Frank seemed really upset.

I gave her a puppy-dog look. "We should make up for the sake of the kid."

"Oh," she shook her head, "you're such a goof."

"She likes me again," I told Frank.

Now, Tiffany laughed. "You're only on probation," she warned.

"You're both on probation," said Frank. "No more fighting."

"Okay," I agreed. "She's worried about Amy. I'm worried about Amy. You're worried about Amy. What'll we do about it?"

Frank knew. "She has to figure out who her friends are."

Tiff regarded him, thoughtfully. "You went through that, didn't you?"

"Uh-huh, and I found out Robby was my friend, not the guys I used to hang with." He looked at me. "Then I met Martin." His eyes were getting moist. "And I have you, Tiff. I'm lucky."

I felt myself misting up, too. Hey, I was touched.

"Oh, my God," Tiffany exclaimed, "not both of you!" It was the strongest expression I'd ever heard her use. We couldn't help laughing at her reaction.

"Did you get anything out of Robby?" I asked Frank.

"I, uh, pretty much filled him in." I'd never doubted that he would. "He couldn't tell me anything." Frank was silent for a moment. "You know, he's always liked Amy," he continued, "even though he didn't show it."

"She knows," said Tiffany.

"Everyone knows." Tiffany raised her eyebrows at me. "You need to be more observant," I chided.

"I suppose," she admitted. "I do tend to be in my own world."

"Yeah, that's *her* thing," claimed Frank. "She's deep."

Tiff thought that was hilarious. Frank looked at me. "I was serious," he said.

"Yeah, I know," I told him, "and it's true, but it still sounds funny."

Tiffany shifted gears. "I'm sorry I blew up at you, Martin."

"No problem," I mumbled. I had a feeling I'd deserved it.

"We should always be friends."

Frank nodded in agreement.

"Frank's right," I said. "We're lucky."

Chapter 32

"The situation's worked out pretty well," said Dad. "I'll admit to having had doubts." He looked over to Frank. "No offense intended, kid."

"It's okay, Mr. Groves. I know what you mean."

"I do miss having Frank at home," Ms. Differs told us, "but yes, it has worked."

"Then everyone's happy with the status quo?" asked Deputy Ortiz. He'd suggested we get together: Frank, his mom, my parents. He hadn't mentioned me but I wasn't about to miss it.

"Frank fitted right in here," said Mom. "He can stay as long as he wants, if his mother approves."

"He eats an awful lot," I offered.

"I know," said Ms. Differs. "Can you afford him?"

"They let me have the table scraps," joked Frank.

"You sound like your father," she sighed. She turned to the deputy. "Doesn't he sound like John?"

Ortiz nodded gravely.

Ms. Differs' smile was slightly sad. "He used to really bug Buddy."

"I didn't have any—discipline, then."

"No, you didn't," she accused. "He never meant anything by it."

Suddenly, Frank said, "If you poke the bear too many times he's gonna turn around and bite you." We all looked at him in surprise; all except Dad. "Mr. Groves told me that one."

"Homespun wisdom, from you?" asked Mom.

"It's a line I'd use in class, sometimes," he explained. "I've seen plenty of kids who needed to learn it."

"If Frank did," decided Ms. Differs, "then I'm glad he was here. But come over more often," she told her son. "At least, I can feed you. And you too, Martin."

~

"Everyone's getting taller," complained Amy. "Everyone but me."

"What brought this on?" I wondered.

"Look at you. You must have grown an inch since I met you while I've stayed the same." She gave me a disgusted look. "It's not fair." Like it was my fault.

"Girls mature earlier," my mother told her. "You're certainly tall enough, dear."

"Two years ago I was taller than Tiffany. Last year we were the same height. Now she's shot past me." Amy shook her head. "She's turning into a model or something."

"Something?" I asked. "Such as?"

"Oh, I don't know—a basketball player," she laughed.

"She can't be much over, what, five-six?"

"And chances are she's leveling off," Mom figured. "I don't think she'll catch Martin."

"She'd like to catch him." Amy made a face at me.

"Is that right? You'll have to tell me all about it."

I went to hide in the kitchen.

Jimi and Frank entered the back door. Billie had delivered her brother, and his drums, the previous evening. We'd let him sleep in this morning.

"I didn't know you were here," said Amy, who'd come back for something or another. "I thought you'd arrive in the afternoon."

"No one to bring me, then. What's for breakfast, Martin?"

"You name it. Do you like French toast?"

"I love French toast," Jimi informed me. "But not with cinnamon. That ruins it."

"No argument, there. You gonna eat again, Frank?"

"Sure. Let's all have breakfast together. Amy, too." He looked out into the restaurant. "It's slowed way down." It was past nine.

"Okay, clean a table for us."

~

I made French toast for Frank and Jimi and browned some sausages, too. There were some sweet rolls left (I don't make those, we buy them), which I set out for Amy and me to nibble.

Amy was the only coffee drinker in the group. "It'll stunt your growth," I kidded her. The guys couldn't figure why we thought that was funny.

"Are you going to practice with us, today?" Frank asked Amy.

"I intend to," she answered. "Theo's house?"

"Uh-huh. Everything's there. Even Jimi's drums."

"We'll expect you," I said. "Tiff and I are even prepared to sing back-up."

"She doesn't like my key."

"Neither do I." F was about the worst possible choice for me. "How about trying C for a change?"

"You'll just have to growl along." She knew I wasn't serious. "Or will you go up and sing falsetto?"

"Wouldn't C be easier for Tiffany to play?" Jimi wanted to know. "Isn't that all the white keys?"

"F's almost as easy," said Frank. "There's only one black." That struck him as funny. "Just like our band."

I gave him a pained expression, but Jimi laughed. "Then F is good," he agreed.

"Yeah, but A or E would be easier on guitar."

"Be grateful she didn't choose something like E-flat," I told him. "And don't get any ideas," I warned Amy.

"That's the price for having vocals," she informed us, smiling.

"At least it's not a problem with our instrumental."

"You really plan to do that surf music thing in the show?" Jimi wasn't completely enthusiastic.

"We know it better than anything else."

"And you get your drum solo," Frank reminded him. "We even worked out a good part for Tiff."

Amy had a question. "Won't you learn more than one song?"

"I vote for 'Gloria,'" Frank announced. Tiffany had suggested it.

"With you on vocals?"

"Sure," he volunteered. "Why not?"

"I don't know it," objected Jimi.

"Come upstairs; I'll play you the CD."

"Aren't you going to help clean up?" I asked.

"Forget it," said Amy. "We'll take care of it."

"Undermining my authority?" I waved Frank and Jimi out the door.

"You didn't believe you actually had any?"

I turned to my mother, going through the morning's receipts. "Mom, make her behave."

She looked up and smiled. "Yes, dear. You're doing a great job, Amy."

~

We were, believe it or not, starting to sound good. Even Amy's singing.

"Won't we need microphones and a PA?" asked Jimi.

"Eventually," I said, "but the school provides them for the show."

Amy seemed interested. "How big should a PA system be?"

None of us were really sure, but Frank felt that it should be stereo and "have plenty of inputs." He promised to show Amy catalogs.

We picked up an audience, mid-afternoon. Jason and a friend came wheeling up on their bikes and watched for a while. His buddy seemed intrigued by Jimi.

"Don't black guys play rap?" he asked Jason.

Jason thought that was funny. "Hey, Frank," he called, "are you gonna do a rap song?"

Frank ignored him, but Jimi said "There will be rappers auditioning. One girl asked me to play for her."

"Will you? We wouldn't mind," Frank let him know.

"Maybe. I'm not much into that hip-hop stuff."

"But you hate to turn down a pretty girl?" I kidded.

"You know it."

Amy looked at her watch. "I have to go home now and get cleaned up."

Frank started to say something but a look from Tiffany kept him quiet. After Amy left, Tiff told us, "She has a date. Earl, again."

Frank made a disgusted noise.

"Hey," I said, "he's an athlete, has a car, and girls, well, think he's good looking?"

Tiffany nodded. "But he's still a jerk."

"And he's stolen Amy away from you."

"I—guess so," Tiff admitted. She was willing to be honest.

"But, then," I reflected, "we've stolen you away from Amy, haven't we?"

"When did he get the car?" asked Frank.

"Last month. His parents gave him one when he turned sixteen." I'd gotten the news from J.R.

It was time for a break, anyway. We went upstairs and sat on the back porch.

"We really should have a second song," Tiffany felt. "Marlon says they'll allow two at the audition."

"How about at the show?" I asked.

"Just one. But it gives us an extra shot."

"It should be completely different," said Jimi. "Different from the one we're already doing."

We all agreed. "We could write something," suggested Frank.

"Giving up on 'Gloria?'" I wanted to know.

"Not necessarily. Let's try working it up."

It wasn't difficult and Frank's squawky, nasal vocals actually sounded okay. At least, they were energetic.

Around four, Mom came by in the SUV. We took Jimi and his

drums back to Blessed, where his father, a quiet man in paint-spattered overalls, thanked us.

I thought it had been a good day. My only concern was Amy.

~

"You aren't going to fish?" asked J.R.

"No. Someone should stay at the Lodge. My mom can't do it all."

"I thought Amy works there."

"Only in the mornings," I explained, "and only in the restaurant."

"You all are worried about her, aren't you?" J.R. became very serious.

"It's really effecting Tiffany. She's a worrier, anyway."

He dropped the weights he had just picked up. "She's not the same Amy, anymore."

"Could Earl have anything to do with it?"

"There's always a boy," observed Mr. Edwards, "but he's usually a symptom, not the cause."

"Then what's with her?" asked J.R.

"Of course, she's not the same Amy. Everyone changes." He looked at his protege. "And everyone tries to make some sense of it. Even you. We all search for who we are."

"And where we belong," I added.

Chapter 33

"Hi, Amy," said Rob.

She only looked up, said "Hi," and returned to her work. Robby continued to the kitchen.

"I wish you could come," he told me and I'm sure he meant it.

"Yeah, I know, man, but you and Frank don't need me along." I shrugged. "I'm not a fisherman, anyway."

Robby nodded. "He and J.R. are loading the boat. Should be a great day."

It seemed a good time to discuss Frank. "You understand why he wouldn't go hunting with you?"

"He spilled."

"Thought he might. Frank's not one to hide his feelings."

Rob became reflective. "I don't think he really even cares about going fishing."

"He just wants to do something with his best friend."

"I think that's you, now."

"Why not both of us?" I asked.

Robby laughed. "Yeah, why not?"

~

"Didn't keep any?" I wondered, "or didn't catch any?"

"We hooked a few," J.R. responded. "They made me throw mine back."

Dad snorted. "It was only a suggestion. The fishing was slow today."

"Robby thinks the water's too warm," Frank informed me.

"Everyone tells me it's unusually mild," commented Dad. "I don't think we'll have a white Christmas, after all."

J.R. shook his head and looked at me. "Two of a kind."

"It's been cold in the North," Rob said. "We'll get a big front eventually."

But it didn't come soon. The weather was still warm when Christmas vacation started.

~

By the last week of school, Amy had stopped riding the bus. I knew Tiff wasn't happy but too much was going on to think about it. Jeff was home and Christmas was a week away.

Tiffany and I also had to concentrate on our concert. The band was pretty sloppy, Wednesday afternoon, performing for the school. Mr. Montero rehearsed us hard on Thursday; we had to be ready that night.

I was riding with the Theos, since band members needed to arrive early. My family would come later, leaving Frank in charge for a few hours. Mom dropped me at their house, dress shirt on my back and flute case under my arm. My tie was in there, too.

"We're waiting for Amy," Tiffany told me. "She wants to come along."

"Didn't she see the concert at school?"

"I think she feels a little guilty," said Marlon. "Guilty about neglecting Tiff."

Earl Johnson dropped her and didn't seem happy about it. I'm sure I heard him use the word "losers." Amy didn't seem very happy, either, but cheered up once we got underway.

We were glad to have her with us, chatting about whatever. It kept us from just sitting there, getting nervous. In no time at all, it seemed, we were at Pinelands High.

Tiffany, as usual, wouldn't wear a dress. Instead, she was in dressy, dark slacks, and a white blouse. No, it was a shirt. She looked classy. Marlon had to don a blazer for conducting. He looked good, too; it suited him. I could have passed for any dork. That's okay. I didn't want to stand out.

We took our places on stage, curtain down as Mr. Montero gave last-minute instructions. Next to me, Billie was carefully arranging her long dress. She seemed to have some jitters; a lot of the kids did. I'd been more nervous the previous day, playing for my peers.

Once the curtain went up, all that disappeared. We did good.

~

My folks had the same friendly disagreement every year. Mom wanted to get the tree up, and down, early. Dad, the traditionalist, preferred the opposite. But we were a business, now; it went up early, in the restaurant.

That Saturday, "The Middle of Nowhere" assembled to rehearse. We figured we'd be too busy to manage it again until after Christmas. The Theo house was strung with lights. A lot of homes near the river had big displays—they made quite a sight from a boat, reflecting across the water.

We just couldn't get into practicing. We'd play a while, then gab a while. The main topics were Christmas plans and Christmas gifts.

Tiffany was curious about Frank's situation.

"I'll spend most of the day with my mom," he told her. "I'm going over early so we can open gifts together."

"Then he'll come back and do the same thing, after we close the restaurant." We didn't expect much traffic on Christmas morning.

"And then," Frank continued, "it's off to Mom's again, for dinner."

"Good thing they're close together," commented Tiff.

"How about church?" asked Jimi. "My family will be in church and then we'll deliver baskets."

"Next thing, you'll tell us Christmas is about *giving*," I joked.

He grinned. "I expect to get my share of presents."

Frank and I left our amps again. With Jeff in the room, we didn't have space for them.

~

A breeze started picking up Sunday, from the South.

"Looks like we're finally going to get that big front," said Dad.

"The weather report says there may be coastal flooding," warned Mom. "Better not leave anything lying on the dock."

By evening, the wind was really heavy and a tad more westerly. I could hear it howling in the night. It made it hard to sleep.

Frank shook me. I couldn't see the clock; the electric had gone out. "Look," he said, pointing to the window. Jeff was already there.

The river was rising rapidly, a spreading sheet of water. It flowed across the low ground and into the shop. Our floating dock was lodged against the shore but all the boats remained attached. There had been occasional rain squalls through the night but right now it was only blowing.

"I'll see if Mom and Dad are awake," said Jeff, wrapping himself in a robe.

Frank seemed entranced. "This is *awesome*."

I had a bad feeling. "It'll be worse down river."

"Our amps!" he wailed.

I found a flashlight and checked my watch. It was nearly two.

Jeff returned. "We're going downstairs. Get dressed," he told us, "and wear something heavy. It's getting cold."

We congregated in the candle-lit restaurant and listened to the radio. There had been a tremendous storm surge all along the coast and it was still coming up as we approached high tide. The combination of an extra-cold front and an extra-warm Gulf had set it off, creating a low-pressure system as powerful as a hurricane.

From the front door, I watched the river lapping at the edge of the road. "Is there anything we can do?" I asked.

Mom shook her head. "We'll have to wait it out." She shivered. "Can we get some heat in here?"

"I'll turn on the oven," said Jeff. It used gas.

"We'll need to do something about the boats," Dad decided, "but not before dawn. It may drop by then."

~

The water did start to subside around daybreak. First, though, it came across Riverside Road. That was scary, but it was still well below us on our hill.

I'm sure I saw a few flakes of snow in the gray light, as the temperature took a nose-dive. The wind had now moved to the

North-west. Jeff brought his camera out and snapped shots from the driveway.

"Want a really great picture?" I asked. "Come with me."

We climbed to the tree house. From that vantage, it appeared almost as though we were on an island.

"A lot of people have water in their houses," Jeff observed, using up his entire roll of film. Even this far up the river, we must have been six feet above normal high tide. The radio was saying ten or more at the coast.

We would have to round up all the boats before the water dropped too much. Those at the dock seemed okay; those kept on land had wandered, trailers dragging behind like anchors. Dad waded to his boat, wearing a wet-suit, and then motored around in what was normally an open field, hauling the wayward vessels into shallower water. There, we made certain they were seated on their trailers. We were done by late morning and the water had dropped by half.

Deputy White stopped by to check on us, once the road was open. He said there'd been a lot of damage, down river and all along the coast. People dead and missing, too.

~

Right then, nothing more could be done, so Frank and I got on our bikes to check the neighborhood. A few houses were low enough to have experienced serious flooding; many more had water rise to a few inches above or below floor level. And a lot of cars had become junk, overnight.

"Here comes your brother."

Jason came pedaling up the muddy street. "Didja see it? Didja see the river?"

"Yeah," said Frank. "It must have been the most incredible thing I've ever seen."

"How's your place?" I asked. "Your mom okay?"

"Uh-huh. Our floor's all wet."

Frank looked at me. "They could come to the Lodge, couldn't they? If the house is too messed up?"

"Sure," I said. "It's gonna be a cold night. A lot of people," it occurred to me, "may need a place to stay."

Chapter 34

"I really thought we were going to die." Tiffany shuddered at the memory.

"Our boat was on its trailer downstairs," Marlon told us. "It floated up and banged against the floor all night. We were afraid it would break through."

We were at the Akin's home. It stood on higher ground. The only water there had come through the roof.

"Daddy's seen flooding before but nothing like this," said Tiff. "Not even in a hurricane."

"He thought we might get a few inches of water so he moved the cars yesterday. Tiff made me bring your amps upstairs, too."

Frank breathed that proverbial sigh of relief.

"Our parents felt we should stay out of the house until it's checked for structural damage," Marlon continued, "so here we are."

"They were lucky," spoke Amy. I was finally seeing her bedroom, pink pillows and all. "Some places were totally destroyed."

"Parker's Restaurant is gone," Tiffany informed us.

Amy nodded. "There will be lots of repair and construction work for a while. It sounds like a terrible thing to say but my dad's going to make money from this."

"I'm just glad we're all safe," was Frank's comment.

~

Amazingly, no one had died in Ruby. Other places along the coast had not been so fortunate.

Many had been displaced, at least temporarily. A shelter was opened at Ruby Elementary but some preferred a motel room, so we filled up, Monday night. Mr. Perry, the head grounds-keeper down at The Mooring, stopped by to say they could take in any overflow we had. And we did have overflow. But by Tuesday, people were returning to their homes. That included Frank's family.

Before they left, my folks made them an invitation.

"Your place may do for sleeping but not for celebrating Christmas," said my dad. "Why don't you come over here?"

Mom added, "At least for dinner."

It didn't take much arm-twisting to get a "yes."

We spent Tuesday cleaning up. The river had left inches of black mud behind, which we hosed, shoveled and broomed away. It looked like the dock would have to be rebuilt and the shop had been gutted but not destroyed. I guess we'd been lucky.

Wednesday was Christmas Eve. Normally, I'd be absorbed in anticipation. This year, there was too much going on. Frank and I, and Jeff as well, decided to bike around town and see the damage. Jeff wanted more photos.

It was bad along the river. Most of the boathouses and docks were gone—any structure that was actually on the river was heavily damaged. Those on the other side of Riverside Road, like the Theos's house, fared better. The community center had collapsed.

I had to see Mr. Edwards's place. I knew it was low, especially the studio. He was inside, trying to clean things up. It was a mess.

"At least my paintings were up high enough," he said. The water mark on the walls was waist-level. "But my cabinets turned over." They were wood, and had floated. All his papers, all his books, were ruined.

"I heard an odd noise in the night," he told us, "and when I stepped out of bed, the water was already ankle deep. It was too late to try to come over here." He shook his head. "We were more worried about saving ourselves. Spent the night sitting on the kitchen counters."

Frank was impressed by that. "Is your house ruined?"

"No, it's concrete. We can just throw out the furniture and start over." He gave a weak smile. "Compared to some, we were lucky."

~

A few families remained at the Lodge that night. It seemed a lousy way to spend Christmas Eve, so Mom and Dad opened the restaurant and set out snacks. We even had Christmas music playing. It was appreciated and made us feel better, too.

We opened up on Christmas morning, as well, but served only coffee and pastry. No one wanted to bother with cooking; we'd be starting dinner, soon enough. Frank set off early for his Mom's house.

And returned, around ten: time for presents.

The usual books, the ugly plaid shirts, the gag gifts (unavoidable in this family) were opened and briefly admired. Then came the biggies.

For Jeff, a stereo; for Frank, a video game system. I was glad to see him get equal treatment. The size and shape of my box suggested only one thing: guitar.

But not the guitar I had expected or hoped for. It was a classical, yes, but electrified, with built-in pickup and cutaway body.

Frank was ear-to-ear grin. "Tiff and I picked it out. Now you can be loud."

It was exactly what I wanted. I just hadn't known it!

Bill brought Ms. Differs and Jason over later. His truck had been up just high enough to avoid damage but her old car was ruined. Before dinner, Mom and Dad took them down to look at the dock; they thought Bill might be interested in some extra work.

But he and Julie Differs seemed to be arguing about something on their way back up the hill. Whatever the problem was, they put it aside during dinner.

"Now I see why Frank likes it here," she said, looking over the feast.

"Yeah, Mom, it was your cooking, all along," claimed Frank.

Before they left, Frank and I cornered Jason, to see if he knew anything.

"Bill wants to leave," he told us. "He's got a job down in Saint Pete and wants us to go with him."

~

Mr. Akin, Amy's father, promised to put us first on his list. With Jeff and Frank and I to help, he and Dad had everything repaired in a few days. Then, at the Lodge, we were back to normal. That wasn't true for the rest of Ruby.

The whole disaster brought back all those misgivings about the place. This time, I thought maybe my parents shared them. What if they decided to pull out?

Or, what if Ms. Differs moved away? Would Frank go with her? I'd never had as close a friend, though we'd known each other less than half a year.

Saturday morning, I suggested to Amy that we could start practicing again.

"Is that all you think about? I have other things to do." She seemed, well, belligerent. "I have a life."

Her vehemence left me speechless. For a moment, she looked uncertain, like she was thinking of apologizing. But she set her jaw and went back to work.

I don't know if I'd ever felt so rotten. This holiday truly had been a disaster: some people lost houses but I was losing friends.

Chapter 35

"She came over here and cried about being such a bad person," Tiffany told me. "But, really, she likes you."

"She got herself all worked up. Maybe—maybe she had to." I was trying to make sense, both to Tiffany and to me.

"To say it?"

"Or even to believe it."

Tiff caught my meaning. "To justify her choice."

"Yeah." That was it, exactly. "But maybe we are a bunch of losers."

Frank gave his assessment. "We may be losers but Amy's just plain lost."

We couldn't disagree with that.

"I handed her the tapes we made and told her to do what she wanted." Tiffany sighed. "Things used to be simpler. It was just Amy and me."

"Life was simpler for all of us, once," I stated, "before I came here."

The regret in my voice surprised Frank. "It's not your fault, man."

Tiff managed a little smile. "Martin's so self-absorbed. He thinks everything's his fault."

I had to smile, too. It was true.

"My life got a lot better with Martin around," said Frank, "and we might never have been friends, Tiffany."

"We're three misfits," I decided, "who finally found a place to fit in."

~

"Looks like you'll be seeing a lot more of me, kid," said Jeff. He was reading something official looking.

"Did you already flunk out?"

"Nope. Guess again."

I thought, this time. "You've—transferred?"

He held up the paper. "Acceptance from the University of Florida."

"Great." Then I wondered, "Why?"

"For one thing, it's cheaper, now that Mom and Dad are Florida residents."

"Hey, that means they plan to stay."

He gave me a curious look. "You thought they might leave?"

"After the flood, I wasn't sure. They seemed pretty discouraged."

"The only discouraged one around here has been you. After all," he continued, "Dad can get his captain's license next month. He wouldn't give up on *that*."

So I'd misread my parents, too wrapped up in my own problems, and put the worst possible interpretation on events.

"You'll have to meet Marlon," I told him. "He knows everything about UF."

~

Everyone got together that Tuesday. Everyone but Amy. Billie brought her brother and stayed, herself. She also brought her flute, saying we should practice our piece at least once during vacation. The two of us ended up giving a little concert for our friends.

We were back to rehearsing in the restaurant. Although the Theos's house had checked out okay, their downstairs was still unusable. It was too cold to be outdoors, anyway.

Jeff was impressed by Billie's playing. "I've hardly touched the flute since high school," he enthused (like that was long ago), "but I may take it up, again." He and Billie and Marlon seemed to hit it off well.

I plugged my new guitar into Frank's amp, which wasn't ideal but worked. It pointed out our need for a PA system.

Even Robby came. He had to show us his new fishing rod and hear our disaster stories. There had been no damage at his place, other than downed trees. Flooding didn't reach that far up the river.

It was the first time he'd heard "The Middle of Nowhere" play.

Mom listened to us awhile. "Ready for a gig?" she asked.

"We don't have enough songs," answered Frank, "especially without Amy."

I suspected that my mom wasn't asking an idle question. "Do you have something in mind?" I inquired.

"We're inviting a few of our new friends over tomorrow night. You should try to get Amy to come." She addressed this directly to Tiff. "Since her parents will be here."

"A New Year's Eve party?" Jimi looked to his sister. "Do you think I could do that?"

"I suppose," she replied. "We did let you stay overnight."

"You're invited, too," Mom let her know. "All of you."

~

So it was on. We figured we'd better learn another song, pronto. Maybe "Auld Lang Syne," I suggested. Tiffany pointed out that we could play that from the sheet music. Better to memorize something else.

As we started going through possibilities, our "audience" became bored. "Let's go for a ride," invited Billie. She, Jeff and Marlon went cruising, but Robby preferred to hang with my dad.

Tiffany tried to contact Amy but she wasn't home. Her mom told Tiff the best time to call back. Mrs. Akin knew Amy might not be willing to phone the Lodge.

We ended up choosing "Summertime Blues" and got it down pretty quickly. Somehow, I let myself be talked into handling vocals. I'd already sort of learned the song and Frank knew I sang it when no one was around.

Once Tiff got Amy on the phone, they talked quite a while. Or, more precisely, Amy talked and Tiffany listened. It was like old times.

"Well," said Tiff, after they hung up, "she's agreed to come. And she says she has a surprise for us."

~

"Isn't that Bill Watson's truck?"

It was later that afternoon and everyone had left except Robby.

"Yeah," said Frank. "I wonder what he wants." He tried to sound cool but we were all apprehensive. What if he was going to take Frank away?

The three of us sat on the dock, watching Bill slowly walk our direction. He looked like a man with something important to say and no words to say it.

"Do you have a minute, Frank? I need to—talk to you."

Frank motioned toward a chair. Bill glanced at Robby and me, then sat. He stared at his feet. "I know," Bill began, and then began again. "I know we haven't got along." He looked up. "All sorts of reasons for that, I 'spose." Bill shook his head. "Aw, hell, Frank," he let it out, "fact is, I'm leavin' and your mother won't come with me. Says this is her home."

He was silent for a moment, before telling Frank "I reckon you're part of the reason she wants to stay, but that's okay. Got nothin' against you." Bill appeared to relax, having stated that. "Wanted you to know it, before I go. Sometimes, things just—" He ran out of words.

"Yeah, they really do," agreed Frank.

"I'll miss that smart mouth of yours, boy." A brief smile crossed his rugged, wind-burned face. "Maybe your mom will follow me after a while." He shrugged. "And maybe she won't."

"Do you have to take a new job?" Frank asked. "Is it more important than—than my mother?"

Bill seemed bemused. "That's what *she* asked." He hesitated. "And I don't know. We might've been headed for a breakup, anyway."

Frank couldn't resist smiling. "You were a bit hen-pecked."

Bill laughed. "She wouldn't even let me have a beer in the

house!" He stood and offered his hand. "I'm on my way. Friends?"

"Sure," said Frank. "Friends," and shook goodbye.

Chapter 36

"I'm off," called Jeff, from the door.

"We've always known it," I told him.

Jeff got into Billie's car, where Marlon and Melissa Parker waited. They were headed for a party in Blessed. Messy's Mustang had been ruined; tonight, she was going along more-or-less as Jeff's date.

Which made Billie Marlon's date, though both would probably deny it.

Frank and I had been getting the restaurant ready, moving tables out of the way. Now, we helped Jimi set up his drums. Tiffany would come later, riding with the Akins.

They were the first guests to arrive. Tiff came in, carrying her keyboard. Amy followed with its stand. The girls waved a "Hi" and immediately returned to the Akins' truck.

A moment later they hoisted out a boxy object. Heavy, too, it seemed—they carried it between them. As they entered, I could see it was an amp, about the size of mine.

Amy was ready to burst, as she proudly displayed it.

"It's a PA!" exclaimed Frank. "Neat."

Indeed, it was an all-in-one system, the sort favored by the guitar-playing, folk-singing coffeehouse crowd.

"You show it to them, Amy," said Tiffany. "I'll get the rest of your stuff." Amy began pointing out features, like she'd been a tech-head all her life. Tiff returned shortly with a microphone stand, tape deck and Amy's ubiquitous tote-bag.

Tiffany motioned me to the side as the others started hooking things up.

"Amy chose it and bought it herself," she told me, "and with her own money. Now she can contribute. She won't feel like we're throwing her scraps."

"It's very nice," I admitted. "Just what we need. But Amy can perform all by herself now, and if she gets mad at us again—"

"She can pick up her PA and leave. I know. She's letting us know she's independent, too."

"Which may be good," I suggested.

Tiff gave her friend a long look. "This could pull us closer together or push us further apart."

~

My parents loved Amy's little amp. It didn't take long for them to patch a CD player into it. We used it all evening.

It was a small party: a half-dozen, not-so-young couples. Although I didn't recognize most of them, the girls could supply names. Only one kid had been dragged along, a middle schooler named Annie. She attached herself to Amy. Given the choices, I'd have done the same.

Robby showed up, too, and was decidedly ill at ease with all these adults. We, the guys, ended up hanging out in the kitchen, where I was helping with the food and drink. Helping? Actually, I'd taken charge.

"I don't know if I like your efficient side," said Rob. "I wouldn't want to work for you."

"He'd fire you before the day was over," Frank informed him. "Me, he'd never hire in the first place."

"Aw, I'm not that bad," I protested.

"Yes, you are," all three insisted.

Tiffany came back. "Ready to perform?" she inquired.

I felt a knot form in my stomach. In here, I was in control; out there, I'd be at the mercy of a roomful of strangers.

Frank asked "What'll we do first?"

"Amy should start things off," I said. "One of the songs we practiced with her."

Tiffany agreed with me. "Great idea. I'll get her."

We'd done a sound-check, of sorts; now we quickly decided on three songs for our first "set." Frank was unanimously chosen MC.

It seemed strange, being so close to our audience. It's very different, up on stage. Once we launched into "San Antonio Rose," the feeling wore off. Our playing was horrendous, though.

Amy sat down by Rob and Annie, and we started our "show piece," "Walk, Don't Run." I thought it came off well; we'd certainly practiced it enough. "Summertime Blues" came last. I managed to get the vocals out (Frank did the low bits) and we got polite applause as Frank said "Thank you" and "we'll be back later."

Then I went into the restroom and puked my guts out.

Frank came in. "Feeling better?" He didn't bother to hide his amusement.

"Yeah. Give me a minute. There may be more." I looked up at him. "You sounded professional."

"Thanks. You did okay, too. I don't think anyone else figured out why you hurried in here."

"You know me too well. I guess that was all." I started washing up. "I should have done that *before* we went on."

"You'll get another chance. Hey, we should do this again next year for the millennium celebration!"

"That's two years away," I replied. I'd had this conversation with others already. "The next millennium starts in Two-thousand One."

"You sure about that?"

"Ask my dad. I don't feel like explaining it all!"

Later, Amy did some numbers with taped accompaniment. She could plug a tape deck in along with her mike. We had Tiffany's keyboard hooked up as well.

Some of the guests couldn't resist doing the karaoke thing. Hearing them made me realize that we actually sounded pretty good. We were worth every penny we weren't being paid.

"The Middle of Nowhere" went on again around eleven-thirty. We played everything we knew, including encores of our first set. At midnight, I took over Frank's guitar and Tiff and I played "Auld Lang Syne." There was plenty of applause but that might have been for the clock.

~

Rob and Jimi stayed the night. It was crowded, and even more so when Jeff came in, around two.

He was the first up in the morning. Jeff needed surprisingly little sleep. He woke me up and we went down to help clean up the mess.

"How'd it go?" I asked him. "Do you like Messy?"

"She seems nice. And she told me to call her Melissa." Jeff didn't sound enthusiastic. "I like Billie better."

"So Marlon has a rival. A sophisticated college boy, no less." I was kidding but, on second thought, I added "It would serve him right."

"I don't know what kind of relationship they have," he replied, "but I'm not cutting in on it. Not yet, anyway. How about your evening?"

"It went okay." We put the last table in place. "Should I unlock the door?" I called to Mom.

"Go ahead. I have all the dirty dishes together." She smiled and looked toward the ceiling. "Time to wake Frank."

"Do you think he'll move back in with his mom, now?" I asked her. It had been on my mind.

"Not right away. Don't tell Frank this," she warned, "but Julie can't stay in that house of hers. It was pretty dilapidated before the flood; now, it's probably unsafe.

"By the way," she continued, "you sounded great last night. Especially *after* you threw up."

~

"Only three days left," lamented Frank.

"This was the strangest Christmas vacation I've ever had," I told my friends. "I may be glad when it's over."

The three of them booed me.

Frank wondered, "When's Billie coming back?" She'd gone off with Jeff and Marlon.

"She's not," said Jimi. "They went to Gainesville. Mr. Groves is taking me and Robby home."

"They went to look at the campus," I elaborated, "and took Messy, uh, Melissa, with them. She's applied for next year."

"Billie plans to go there, too. I don't think I'll go to college," Jimi informed us. "I'm too dumb."

"Let's face it," Rob remarked, "Martin's the only college material here."

I didn't agree with that but figured it wasn't important. They'd have plenty of time to decide.

I had only one thing to say: "Wherever we end up, we should still be friends."

Chapter 37

"Amy has a new confidante."

"So she's finally dumped you?" I asked Tiff, not very seriously.

"More like, added a back-up. Remember Annie?"

I showed my surprise. "The little girl at the party?"

"Yep." Tiffany laughed. "She thought Amy was about the greatest thing she'd ever seen."

"Sorta like you and Jody?"

She groaned. "No, Amy encourages her. I'm—well, I'm kind of mean to Jody."

"Not actively. You simply ignore her."

"Uh-huh. I still don't know what Amy will do at the show," sighed Tiff, looking out the bus window. "And I'm afraid to ask. If I pressure her, she may just get angry."

"No pressure," I agreed, "and no guilt. I think she's been avoiding you because she feels guilty. Then she feels guilty because she's avoiding you!"

"She ought to feel guilty," Tiff said. "She's certainly made me feel guilty about neglecting her."

"It seems more like she's neglected you."

"She always did that. I was the dependable side-kick."

"So she's gone out and found a new one?"

"Looks that way," Tiffany admitted, "but she'll never measure up to the original."

~

"Here's what Shawn told me," Billie reported. "This Johnson boy had been pushing your friend Robby around."

"I guess his new muscles didn't help," I commented.

"He doesn't have the attitude to go with them. Those two do not like each other." She looked at Tiff. "We all know why, huh?"

She went back to her story. "Anyway, before it turned into a real fight, Shawn stepped in." Billie smiled. "Not 'cause he likes Robby. He just can't stand Earl. And," she added, "it was the right thing to do."

"Earl would never leave it at that," said Marlon.

"No. There's gonna be a fight after school. You can depend on it."

~

"I had to stay," said Robby.

"Of course," I agreed. "So what happened?" Rob had ridden home with J.R. the previous afternoon.

"Shawn *pulverized* Earl. When his buddies didn't like that, J.R. stopped them from getting involved."

"I wish I'd seen." Frank sounded heartbroken.

"You can," chuckled Robby. "Some guy videotaped the whole thing."

One question gnawed at me. "What did Amy think of all this?"

"She seemed pretty disgusted with Earl." Robby shrugged. "But she rode home with him."

"Hey, Amy's at her stop!" Frank exclaimed.

Mrs. Cannon spoke. "Don't pry, boys. Give her some time."

So we only said "Hi" and Amy took her old seat. Without showing the slightest surprise, Tiffany boarded and sat down beside her. Eventually, they started whispering.

By the time we reached school, Amy actually smiled.

~

Amy wasn't on the bus that afternoon. She had cheerleader practice and would ride home with J.R.

It was only a week till the talent show auditions. We needed to concentrate on rehearsing. Then we'd have to concentrate on midterms.

"It's A through L on Monday," Marlon told me. "That's you, Mr. Groves. The rest on Tuesday."

"Amy will be on Monday, then. How about my duet?" I'd asked.

"Tuesday. We have you under 'Peale.' Amy's the first act on our list."

185

And we still didn't know if we'd be backing her.

Frank and I rode over to Tiffany's house. "Earl was 'under the weather' today," Tiff told us. "Both eyes swollen shut." She didn't seem unhappy about it.

Tiffany wouldn't share any of Amy's confidences, but it didn't matter. Amy herself showed up, seeking her support system.

She plopped down on the end of Tiffany's bed. "I've about had it with Earl. Now he blames J.R. for not helping him!"

Tiff's voice was full of frustration. "Oh, Amy, you knew what he was like."

"Sure." Amy half-smiled. "He's an obstinate, stuck-up—oaf. But he's my oaf. You have two guys following you around."

Tiffany looked Frank and me over. "I'll let you have one of them. Which do you want?"

"Oh, pick me, pick me," sang Frank, waving his arm and cracking us up.

It seemed as good a time as ever. "We are rehearsing tomorrow," I told Amy, "if you want to come."

"Okay," she agreed. She did not commit to anything more.

~

As we left, Frank commented to me "I never thought Amy'd be jealous of Tiffany over boys."

"Yeah, like you really believe that."

He laughed. "We're not in her league anymore. She's moved up to athletes."

"Or thinks she has," I observed, "or thinks she's supposed to have?" I was confusing myself. "But she is jealous of Tiffany."

Frank gave me a sharp look. "How so?"

"Because Tiff's become successful on her own. She was always in Amy's shadow before, right?"

"Always. I hardly noticed her there."

"Amy needs to accept the changes in her friend—or they won't be friends." I stopped myself. "Do I make sense or just sound pretentious?"

"Both," was his impression, "sort of like your dad." He thought that was funny.

"Then Amy's, like, competing with Tiff?" Frank conjectured. "Trying to outdo her?"

"I'd say so. And Earl's there for showing off."

"The trophy boyfriend!"

"He wouldn't like to hear that."

"Can I tell him?" he pleaded. "Hey, are we trophies, too?"

"Maybe," I admitted.

The idea made him think seriously. "Tiff and Amy may be competing," Frank agreed, "but they're playing different games."

~

Billie Peale was angry. Fortunately, she wasn't angry at me. On the way to Ruby, her car had been egged.

"I saw who it was: Earl Johnson and his cronies. And I saw you, girl," she glared at Amy, "scrunched down in the back seat."

"I—I didn't—" Amy burst into tears and fled to the restaurant.

"Give her a couple of minutes," said Tiff, matter-of-factly. "Do you think it was because you're Shawn's friend?"

"Or ours?" I wondered.

"Who knows?" Billie scowled. "I don't care and I don't think they care. What's worse," she went on, "they were bullying Jimi at school. I can't have that."

"I'll go talk to Amy now. Maybe this'll put some sense into her," Tiffany hoped.

"I'd like to knock some sense into her empty blonde head." We may have looked apprehensive. "Aah, don't worry; I won't hurt the little twerp." Billie smiled a rather ferocious grin. "I'll go with you," she told Tiff. "We can play good cop-bad cop."

Chapter 38

Robby was thinking career. "I could be a wildlife officer," he said, "or even Marine Patrol."

"How about forest ranger?" suggested Frank. "They don't get shot at."

"Good point," admitted Rob. "Any of them beats welding."

"Do you think Deputy Ortiz has ever been shot at?" I asked.

Frank knew. "Not just shot *at*. He's been hit." He paused dramatically. "He said it left a big bruise under his bullet-proof vest."

"Oh." I was a bit disappointed. "I guess maybe he has a shot at your mom, now."

"Maybe."

"How's she getting to work?" inquired Robby. Ms. Differs was employed at the small local market.

"She finds rides. People are helping each other a lot since the storm."

"It'll wear off." I was feeling cynical.

Amy, once again, did not ride the bus. The hopes I'd had disappeared, but only for a few minutes.

"She's riding with J.R." Tiffany told us. "She wanted to talk with him."

I was relieved. "At least she isn't with Earl."

"She looked mad when you left, yesterday. At you?" Frank asked Tiffany.

"At herself," I guessed.

Tiff nodded at that. "Sometimes I think you understand Amy better than I do."

"You need to get in touch with your feminine side," I kidded her.

"Maybe so," she laughingly agreed. "Your mom seems to connect with her. She and Amy had a talk while we practiced."

"She's had experience dealing with Martin," cracked Frank. "He cries nearly as much as Amy."

"Watch it," I warned him, "or I'll make *you* cry."

~

"If you play like that tomorrow, we'll get Fs."

"I'll be okay." Billie lowered her flute. "Did I scare Amy?"

"Is that what's bothering you?" I asked.

"Among other things." She sighed. "If I go 'round scaring little girls, I'm no better than that Johnson boy."

I couldn't help myself. "You scare a lot more than little girls."

"Yeah. I don't mean to."

"It's just who you are," I offered. "You assert yourself."

"Oh?" She smiled at my assessment. "That doesn't sound too bad."

"Okay," I said. "Just maybe you assert yourself too much. Sometimes."

Now she laughed. "Only sometimes?"

I tried to be serious. "You're a good person, Billie. You know that."

"Thanks for reminding me. I was—" An impish grin crept onto her face. "I was starting to sound like you."

"You're way too upbeat to ever pull it off," I assured her.

~

"I want you to play for me." I sensed the uncertainty behind Amy's words. "If you're still willing."

I tried an encouraging smile. "We've always been willing." There I was, speaking for the band, again. I'd never wanted to be a leader but kept ending up in the role. "What decided you?"

"Marlon told me the judges frowned on taped music." She turned to Tiff. "But I think you put him up to it."

Tiffany kept a straight face but I couldn't contain my amusement. "It sounds like her."

"Actually," Amy said, "it was so much fun on New Year's Eve, I pretty much decided then." She heaved a really deep one. "But then this week was such a disaster."

"Oh, Amy." Tiffany put her arm around her friend. It's true. Right there on the bus. Tiffany!

"I gave Earl an ultimatum." She seemed to like the sound of the word.

Tiffany's voice had a edge to it. "About time."

"You're always so impatient with me, Tiff."

"I'm sorry. It's only because *you're* so stubborn. Especially about Earl."

"I thought I needed him. I didn't have you anymore."

Amy knew how to get to her. Tiffany was feeling guilt, deserved or not; it was her nature.

She went on. Once started, Amy Akin was hard to stop. "You kept telling me what I should do but not how to do it. Mrs. Groves showed me I had options."

This sounded familiar. "Oh, no," I gasped, "Not the 'plan of action.'"

Amy laughed and nodded. "What's that?" asked Tiff.

"My mom's big on sitting down and writing out a battle plan before starting anything. Goals, options, assets, all that. You should have seen the one she made before we moved here!" I didn't tell them but I sometimes did it myself.

Tiff looked at her with surprise. "You worked one out?" I think we all tended to underestimate Amy.

"Uh-huh." Amy had a certain self-satisfied air to her. "But I'm not telling you about it. Except that my biggest asset is J.R."

She added, after a moment's thought, "And you guys. Win or lose, I'm with you."

~

"All Amy really needed to know was that she was in control. She has plenty of natural confidence." Frank and I had to hear what my mom had told Amy. "Once she put it on paper, she realized how many things she had going for her. Things other than Earl Johnson."

"Martin thought Earl was mostly for showing off."

"Hmph." Mom clearly felt that was ridiculous. "Just like a boy. Earl was for her own benefit, to prove her value to herself."

I knew Mom was right but I think I was, too. So I went elsewhere. "I bet having Annie around these past few days didn't hurt. That had to make her feel better."

"Yes, it might have boosted her self-esteem. There's nothing like a little hero-worship." She looked at the two of us with a knowing smile. "Like you get from Frank."

Frank and I thought that was silly but it made us uncomfortable.

"We're friends," I protested. "Equals."

"I like Martin but I don't worship him," Frank assured her.

"If you say," Mom laughed. She didn't sound convinced. "Amy isn't the only one with more confidence," she continued. "You boys, and Tiffany, have grown too."

~

"They like us. They really like us," I whispered to Billie.

"Shut up," she whispered back.

Billie hadn't been nervous at all. She was used to performing in front of the class. I'd been shaking.

"Excellent," Mr. Montero told us, as we returned to our seats. "Good luck in the show."

"If we play like that, we'll need it," Billie told me.

"Practice tomorrow at the Lodge?"

"Okay."

Chapter 39

"Then I told Earl that if he didn't behave, I'd turn J.R. loose on him." Amy giggled. "My cousin, the enforcer."

"J.R.'s willing to do that for you?" asked Billie.

"Not just for me. Robby's his friend, and Martin, too."

"He was getting pretty fed up with Earl, anyway," I noted.

"Yes," said Amy, "J.R. liked the idea. But I don't believe Earl is hopeless. I let him know that I *might* be his girlfriend again, if he straightened up."

"Well, he's not gonna find a better one," Billie declared.

"That's for sure," agreed Tiff.

Annie just looked at her with adoring eyes.

"Yeah, you're wonderful," Frank told her. "Can we practice now?"

Three hours later, we figured we were as ready as we'd ever be. We'd concentrated on Amy's performance. Ours was already well rehearsed.

"After we play on Monday afternoon," suggested Jimi, "you can leave your equipment at my house. We could practice there."

Naturally, we all looked to Billie. She nodded okay.

~

A red mini-van pulled into the drive. "Here's Mrs. Theo," called Frank. Tiffany's mom had volunteered to drive us to school. I was somewhat surprised to see Melissa Parker and Marlon riding along with Tiff and Amy.

"My insurance just came," said Melissa. "I'll have a new car, soon." Her smile hinted of mischief. "Tell Jeff I'll give him a ride." My brother had left for Gainesville in his old junker.

Marlon eyed our equipment. "I'd recommend locking it in one of the band rooms until audition time."

"How many jurors today?" I asked, as we got underway.

"Just three, plus Miss Clarke, our advisor. If she thinks you're objectionable, she'll veto you." He scowled comically. "So behave, Frank."

"Maybe we shouldn't do 'Gloria,'" said Tiffany.

Marlon shrugged. "If you pass, it'll be on that instrumental thing you do."

"If we pass?" Tiff was indignant. "We'd better."

"You'll need a manager if you're good," Melissa joked, "and I'm temporarily unemployed." Parker's Restaurant was already being rebuilt.

"She sounds like your mom," Frank told me.

"Yeah," I agreed. "Think we can trust her?"

"No way," advised Marlon. "I'm pretty sure you and Billie will pass your audition. You sounded good on Friday."

"Aren't you prejudiced, Marlon?" asked Mrs. Theo.

"Probably, Mom, but that's why we have three jurors."

~

School let out at two-thirty. Auditions followed immediately. We set up quickly, Amy sang her two songs, and that was it.

"Thank you," said one of the panelists.

"Don't call us, we'll call you," cracked Marlon.

I thought we did okay but the choices wouldn't be posted till Wednesday. "Good job," I told Amy, as we gathered up our stuff. "See you guys later."

They wished me luck and took off, leaving me with my guitar. I got to watch some of the other acts as I waited. I was not impressed.

They reached the Gs, eventually. I turned out what I thought a decent rendition of "Aura Lee." That was the only piece I intended to perform.

Then I heard Marlon's voice. "Martin's second selection will be a vocal, 'The Rebel Soldier,'" He was loud enough that everyone could hear. "Go ahead, Groves."

I seriously considered getting up and leaving. I semi-seriously considered murdering Marlon. But I really had no choice. I had no chance to get nervous, either. That was, no doubt, the plan. I sang.

After the auditions, Marlon and I walked to the Peales' house.

It stood only a couple blocks from the rear of the school, across an old railroad grade. That was close enough that I could easily carry my guitar. Billie had already taken our equipment in her car.

"Who else was in on that?" I asked him. "Tiff?"

"Everyone was in on it. Even Miss Clarke," he admitted, "and I'm glad we were. It was much better than your first song. You put some emotion into it."

~

"We've unanimously voted," announced Frank. "We're doing 'Summertime Blues' tomorrow."

"It can't be unanimous," I informed him. "I wasn't here."

"I voted for you," said Billie.

"Aah, whatever." I'd been manipulated enough for one day. "Hey, J.R., didn't expect to see you."

"My mom's giving the girls a lift home so I'm waiting here."

Someone else I hadn't expected to see was Shawn Curtiss. He was there with a girl named Angela, one of Billie's friends. They watched as we took a brief, low-volume rehearsal. It was quite a crowd to jam into the Peales' living room.

"We're used to it," said Billie. "There's always someone visiting. Not a bunch of white kids, usually."

"How's your Gramma keeping us all straight?" I wondered. "Should we wear name tags?"

"Behave. Somehow, she's under the impression you're a nice boy."

"Okay. You'll bring our stuff to school tomorrow?"

"Yeah. Make sure you help me unload it."

J.R. broke in. "It's time we left." Both our rides, his mom and mine, were picking us up at the school. "You coming, Shawn?"

"Right there, Junior." Shawn refused to call him J.R.; I think he liked to rub in their height difference. "See you tomorrow, Angela. You, too, Billie."

"We're giving Shawn a lift home," J.R. explained, "but it's a good idea to stick together, anyway."

194

Shawn laughed. "I gotta watch out for my little buddy."

"Don't you dare pat me on the head," J.R. warned him.

Amy seemed surprised. "Would you need help with Earl?"

"He has friends," Shawn pointed out.

J.R. concurred. "I don't think Earl wants to take either of us on but with them pushing him—and each other—anything could happen."

We crossed back to the school. It was starting to get dark, and cold, but our rides were waiting.

~

Auditions again. We took our turns: first, "The Middle of Nowhere," then, Billie and I. They must have been sick of seeing me by the end.

We rode home in the Theos's van. Although the official results would be posted the next morning, Marlon assured us we'd all made it.

He went through his notes. "'Amy Akin and Band'—you should have a name, you know—will do 'Forget Me.' 'San Antonio Rose' didn't cut it."

"You preferred our original?" asked Tiffany.

"Doesn't surprise me," Amy said. "You guys couldn't play Western Swing if your lives depended on it."

"Martin, you have to sing again."

I nodded. I'd expected it.

"But not with the band. We chose 'Walk, Don't Run.'"

Everyone had expected that.

"And Martin and Billie will do their piece, even though we had one vote against." He sounded apologetic. "Susan Koos thought it was boring."

"Should we call Billie and Jimi," I asked, "or make them sweat?"

Chapter 40

"Looks like it was pretty hard *not* to make the cut," remarked Jimi, going down the list. At least two-thirds of the acts had made it.

"How about your friend?" I asked him. She had performed very last at the auditions.

"She's in. Must've been my drumming."

"There were some really bad rappers," said Frank. "I guess it's harder than it looks."

I agreed. "Especially if you write your own."

"Who's judging this, anyway?" Jimi asked.

Frank told us, "I hear that one judge is a DJ. I don't know what station."

"Yeah, and a teacher," I said, "and a student. But none that were on the jury."

~

Frank noticed it first. "What's with the trailer?"

"Beats me." Why would my folks have a mobile home delivered without telling us? But there it was, across the road from the motel.

Dad greeted us with, "Ready to move furniture? It'll be easier before it's put on stilts." I'd seen them do that; they jack the trailer up first, then install piling underneath.

"Who's moving in?" asked Frank.

"Your mom," was the answer. Dad grinned. "She's renting until your house can be fixed up. We got it cheap: flood damage."

"You can stay here and move home at the same time," I told Frank.

"How long?" he inquired.

"A month or two. As long as needed."

I pretended shock. "Mom didn't demand a lease?"

"No need," Dad replied. "We have her first-born child."

I think Frank might have preferred to have his family further away. But things can't stay the same forever.

~

"This is the program," said Marlon, handing Tiffany a sheet of paper. Billie and I crowded in to see it.

"We're near the end," Tiff pointed out.

"And we're near the beginning," said Billie.

"Here's Amy, toward the middle. What is 'Take Aim?'" Tiff asked.

"Must be us." I looked at Marlon. "What's with that?"

"Amy's idea. It's kind of cute, I think. Now, remember," he told us, "get here early if you want a decent sound-check."

~

"Do you think I really need four changes of clothes?" They took up as much space as my equipment. We were jammed into the SUV: me, Frank, Tiff, Amy and my mom at the wheel.

"Absolutely," said Mom.

"Don't get sick and splatter them," Frank advised. "What are we waiting for?"

"Your brother. He wanted to help you."

"Oh, great."

"Don't feel so bad," Tiff laughed. "Amy's parents are bringing Annie."

Jason came running and squeezed in. "Mom's gonna come too," he announced. "She's got a date."

"Who?" demanded Frank.

"Dunno."

We arrived early, as Marlon had recommended, got ourselves set up, and then had some time to kill.

"Let's find something to eat," suggested Billie. "Marlon, keep an eye on our stuff."

He saluted and returned to the business of organizing a show.

We chose one of two fast-food places within a block of Pinelands High and filled a couple of tables. I wisely limited myself to a soda and a package of crackers.

"There's Earl," hissed Tiff. He and a friend took a booth across the room. Now and then, he would give us a look. Finally, he got up and walked over.

"Hi, Amy," Earl said. "Good luck tonight."

~

"A little secret," Marlon said in a low voice. "We're giving out a lot of awards. One of you is bound to get something."

"We intend to sweep, baby," Billie let him know.

The MC announced "Mellow-Dee." That was Jimi's friend and her name really was Melody. Melody Walker. She was a plain girl, the sort that would go in one eye and out the other. Loud, though.

"We're next," Billie whispered. "You okay?"

This time, I was fine. She was the nervous one. "Sure," I told her. "Do you think she's any good?" I inclined my head toward Miss Walker.

"So-so. Aren't you finished tuning?"

The "Gymnopedie" is a lovely piece of music. We knew it would get the applause, not us. So, we did our best and were satisfied. I had to remove my white shirt now and switch to Western clothes. In the restroom, I ran into Jimi, doing the same.

"We are two of the sorriest cowboys I've ever seen," he commented, gazing into the mirror.

"Let's hope everyone's eyes are on Amy."

Tiffany and Frank, on the other hand, looked great; they were made to wear jeans. Amy's choice for the evening had been a flouncy, white tent of a dress, the sort one of her country heroines might wear, until Tiffany told her she looked like a rhinestone-studded blimp. Tiff could be a harsh critic but Amy respected her judgment. The cowgirl look she settled on was much better—especially, the short skirt.

She was cute and she was lively and she sang okay and we played okay. The crowd liked Amy and I'm sure Amy liked the crowd. Jimi and I tried to stay in the background.

Then, another costume change. Mom had surprised me with a

Confederate soldier's jacket. I thought that was corny but I wore it.

Maybe it helped me find the mood. I know I started off too tentatively. Once I got into it, I think the audience did, too.

Afterwards, the emotions hit me. If I'd had anything in my stomach, I would have lost it. As it was, I went into the restroom and heaved a bit. My friends soon followed.

"I brought your clothes," said Frank, with just a hint of a smirk.

"Thanks. Can you guys see anyone in the audience?" I took the Hawaiian shirt he offered me.

"Too dark," Frank reported. "I have no idea who's out there."

"Me, neither. Hey, man," I called to Jimi, "don't tuck it in. No self-respecting Hawaiian would." Or so Mr. Edwards had assured me. It was too "California," he said.

"It'll hide your spare tire, too," Frank told him.

A few minutes later, we were on.

~

The point is to perform, whether making music, telling jokes, or twirling a baton. That's a talent show's purpose and that's enough for me.

Despite that, we listened nervously as the awards were announced. Billie took a deep breath as they called "Best Duo," but it wasn't us.

"Maybe we'll get 'Best Classical Music,'" I told her.

She laughed. "We were the only classical music, idiot."

"'Best Original Song:' 'Forget Me.'"

Frank grabbed Tiff and me and pulled us out on stage to get our certificate. That one had been totally unexpected.

Then, down the list of awards. "Best Group" went to four guys doing a "boy band" thing. We were disappointed but, immediately after, "The Middle of Nowhere" was called out for "Best Instrumental." Another loss for Billie.

"Best Singer," both male and female, went by. I felt sorry for Amy. I really thought she had a shot. Some "Special Awards" came next. Each judge named a favorite. Mrs. Sandeau, the faculty representative (and my English teacher) picked Billie and me. At least one person liked us.

That was followed by a "Special Jury Award" from the audition panel. They chose me. Snobby, intellectual kids—I love 'em.

"No one's being named twice," noted Billie. "They're spreading out the awards."

The only one left was the grand prize: "Best Talent."

And it was Amy.

Chapter 41

"I couldn't have done it without you," Amy told us.

"Darn right," Tiffany agreed.

We'd had our pictures taken, got our equipment together and were out looking for responsible adults to take us home.

"That was great!" Jason had suddenly appeared. "Can I play in your band?"

"Why don't you start your own?" Amy asked him.

"Good answer," Tiff whispered to me.

I whispered back, "Maybe she's trying to find Annie a gig."

"Is Mom here?" Frank asked his brother.

"Yeah. She's with Buddy." Buddy Ortiz had finally dated the girl of his dreams. It only took him twenty years.

"Here's Papa's truck," said Billie. "Let's get your drums loaded, Jimi." As we helped with that, Robby's family walked over.

"Very good, young lady, very good," Mr. Dell congratulated Amy.

Robby told Frank and me, "You've all gone up a notch in Dad's eyes. He loves his country music."

"They were good, weren't they?" asked Fred Akin. We had become surrounded by adults, gushing over us. Frank's mom had to hug him.

My mom just said, "I'd better get you out of here before it all goes to your head. Who's riding with us?"

~

There was school the next day. What a letdown. We didn't even know what to talk about on the bus.

"Why don't you come sit with me and my friends?" Marlon invited at lunch. "You know you'd be welcome." He moved on to his customary spot.

"Should we consider it?" I asked Tiff.

"Why? We know we don't belong there."

"Our public would never forgive us." I looked down the table.

Tiffany gave me a smile. "It would be cruel to desert them."

"Yeah, I've almost started thinking of them as our friends."

"Maybe they are," Tiffany said. "In their way. I guess Marlon still believes I should follow in his footsteps."

"He sees both of us that way. And," I had noticed, "so do some of the teachers."

"Not to mention my mom."

I laughed. "My mom knows better."

"We've found our place, haven't we?" Tiff liked the idea. "Let's stay."

"It's a good place," I agreed, "for now."

~

"Just the man we were talking about," said Mr. Edwards.

"Something good, I hope." So I can't always come up with fresh lines.

"Earl Johnson thinks you stole his girlfriend." J.R. laughed at my expression. "Not you, specifically. It was a group effort." I guess we had been competing with him.

Mr. Edwards told me, "He was just here to patch things up with J.R."

"And to lift," added the Akin boy. "We may never be buddies but there's no reason the two of us can't get along."

"There's the minister's son."

I had to smile. "I can't see him turning the other cheek."

J.R., under his jock persona, was seriously religious. "I would if I thought it would help. But not with Earl."

"Maybe he'll change," I suggested. "People do." Deputy Ortiz came to mind. Had he been like Earl, once?

"Yeah, they sure do," agreed J.R.

~

"We should celebrate our six-month anniversary," decided Dad.

"It's past six months since the two of us first came down," I reminded him.

"Or, if you count from the time we moved, it's another month," said Mom.

Dad waved aside our objections. "I was figuring from the time we signed the papers. The Lodge has been ours for six months."

"It seems like a lot longer." I assumed a puzzled expression. "We used to live in Atlanta, didn't we?"

"Hey," said Frank, "if you have a party, you'll need a band."

"No music until after midterms," I insisted. "We can use the break."

"We'll forget how to play," he grumbled.

"You couldn't play at all when I moved here." When I thought about it, the past half-year had been pretty amazing. "You know, you've really changed."

"All of us have. Look at Tiffany!"

"Amy, too. Shoot, just about everyone we know."

"And you," asserted Frank. "You've changed most of all."

"Me?"

Mom nodded agreement. "You've been so busy with your friends you haven't noticed. You never used to get involved."

"Always just an observer," Dad remarked.

"Now, you're someone who makes a difference," she continued. "And I was afraid moving out here to 'the middle of nowhere' might make you go further into your shell."

"Not with me around," said Frank.

~

So that's how it went: from loser and loner to all-around cool guy in six months. Okay, a little cooler, anyway, and definitely not a loser. I was a finder.

I'd found friends. I'd found a place where I belonged. And I'd found myself, in the middle of nowhere.

AFTERWORD

This is a work of fiction. Any resemblance of the characters to real people is, as they say, purely coincidental. But if any of them seem like real people, then I reckon I've done a decent job.

Ruby is not a real place either but it has similarities to several small villages that lie along the Gulf Coast of Florida between Tampa and Apalachicola. It is also, as the narrative states, not too far from Gainesville so that does narrow it down a little.

Nor is the Hilltop Lodge real. It has a resemblance to a certain now-disappeared little motel I once knew. I lived across the street from that one and my studio at that time was known as the Hilltop Studio. That would be origin of the name. The actual physical description of the Lodge comes from a completely different motel in another town.

When did all this take place? I've chosen to set it in 1998 and 1999. The exact year didn't matter that much, though with the rapid advances in electronics one must watch for anachronisms! The story is, therefore, pre-Face Book, pre-texting phones, pre-much of what became common since.

There was a very real storm like the one in this book back in 1993 (the so-called Storm of the Century) but it was not the same storm. That one came in early March, whereas the mythical storm here arrived in December.

Stephen Brooke is a writer, artist, musician and surfer, living in in an old farmhouse in northern Florida. *The Middle of Nowhere* was his first novel, but he has published several more since it first appeared. This book was written for a young adult audience but, we hope, offers something for everyone. Some of the characters reappear in the adult 'Cully Beach' mystery novels.

http://stephenbrooke.com

www.ingramcontent.com/pod-product-compliance
Lightning Source LLC
Chambersburg PA
CBHW060400030726
47497CB00003B/790